KEVIN

The Invisible Little Boy

KEVIN MCNEIL

D1303274

CONTENTS

Kevin

"Kevin... KEVIN!"

The sudden yelling of his name yanked Kevin from his daydreams and back into his small, dark bedroom. The boy often sat at the edge of his bed lost in thought when he should have been getting ready for school.

His mother shouted again from another room.

"Kevin, hurry up or you will be late, again!"

He grabbed his bag and walked past the adjacent room where his older brother was still snoring. *So unfair.*

Kevin's mother forced him through the tall iron gates each morning, while his brother, who dropped out of school, slept late.

Walking toward the front door, he straightened his shoulders and tried to build up the courage to ask his mother for lunch money. Before he could ask, she was ripping open an envelope from the phone company and moaning like getting news of a death in the family.

Kevin hurried out the door, hoping to miss both his first class and Kenny, the bully who liked to wait for him in the hall. Like every other morning, Kevin took the same route to school. It gave him the shivers. Last year, Kevin had been walking along the very same path when a man dragged him by the collar and *things happened*. He couldn't stand thinking about it for very long, but the memories haunted Kevin each time he crossed the railroad tracks opposite the school's football field. No one knew what had happened to him, and he was sure no one wanted to know. He was already ridiculed by everyone, so he thought: *imagine if they found out my first sexual experience was with some middle-aged creep in a plaid shirt.*

As Kevin took a shortcut through the fence, he saw the bleachers where *it* happened. He quickened his pace and turned the other way, avoiding the curious glances of some students also cutting their classes.

Kevin entered the building, turned the corner, and walked straight into Kenny.

Not today.

Before the jerk could grab him, Kevin ducked under his hefty arms and ran down the hall to his second class, sliding through the door just in time for the roll call.

As he sat down, Aleena, a tall girl with eyes like a cat, yelled across the room, "Ugh, it's Kevin!"

The whole class burst into laughter, including the teacher.

Kevin sat looking down and swallowing the hard lump in his throat. As this was a daily occurrence, there was no reason to let it get to him on this morning. His mother remained ignorant of what he faced each day at school as he was good at keeping it all bottled inside. But at times, Kevin wished he could just disappear and often dreamed of being invisible; and today was no different.

"Kevin, care to tell us why you're late?" Aleena said.

Kevin buried his head in a book and did not respond. When the bell finally rang, Kevin's shoulders slumped in relief—*the end of another long day.* He grabbed his bag and headed for the rear doors to the football field. This was the quickest way out of the building and allowed him to escape with minimal notice. He daydreamed as he walked, his thoughts once more drifting into his favorite fantasy: *being invisible.* He imagined how he would sneak up behind Kenny and strangle him. To the rest of the world, it would look like the fat jerk was choking on one of his

bologna sandwiches. This very thought made Kevin smile.

While daydreaming, he didn't notice the large rock in his path. He stepped clumsily on it, fell, and his books and bag went sprawling across the lawn. Embarrassed, he got up and began gathering everything as quickly as possible. He stood, dusted himself off, and frowned at his bloodied knee. Kevin continued home, but soon noticed his math book was missing. He quickly looked around, sweeping his eyes across the grass and concrete. And then, there it was, right under the stadium bleachers just meters away. Recovering it seemed almost impossible.

Thanks a lot, God.

Kevin was tempted to leave it and keep walking, but his mom would have a fit if she had to buy a new one. So, taking a deep breath, he strode over to the bleachers. Memories assaulted his senses, and he couldn't tell if the dark silhouette in the corner a figment of his imagination was real, or just. When the shape moved, Kevin's heart nearly stopped. He dropped the math book and stared at the man without saying a word. The man looked back at him but did not speak. Remembering his own purpose, Kevin grabbed the math book and sprinted back into the light.

Retreating into his house, Kevin smelled his mother's delicious fried chicken. He had managed to survive another day, but even eating brought him little pleasure. For reasons he couldn't understand, Kevin was afraid to do the most normal things, like eating in front of his family. The thought of them finding something odd in the way he chewed or swallowed sent him running up the stairs to his room with his dinner in hand. He then closed his door and ate in peace. When his plate had been scraped clean, Kevin sat on the bed pondering how he could become less visible (*i.e., invisible*). The image of the silent, strange man crept back into his thoughts. Who was he, and why had he been hiding under the bleachers?

The next day, Kevin shuffled past the bleachers, only this time he didn't cast his eyes in the opposite direction. Instead, he stared deep into the shadows, trying to make out the figure. In a dark corner towards the rear of the space, Kevin thought he saw him. It wasn't the same man who had attacked him, but another man who looked sad and scary...homeless. Kevin thought about approaching the man but was too afraid.

The following day, the man was still there, sitting in the same position. Intrigued and repulsed all at once, Kevin walked a little closer.

He was terrified but found courage in speaking loudly.

"Sir, are you hungry?"
The man glanced up but did not respond.

Kevin's spoke again. "Sir?"

When the man continued to stare, Kevin shrugged and began to walk away, assuming he was too deaf or drunk to answer. He'd only taken a few steps when two strong hands grabbed his shoulders.

"Wait!"

Kevin struggled frantically and screamed. He was certain that he was about to be hurt once again, but the man had clamped a dirty hand over his mouth.

"Shut up, kid!"

The man's eyes were wild, and Kevin stayed quiet.

"Is it true? Can you see me?"

The boy blinked at him in confusion, and then the man released him.

"Sir, are you crazy?" Kevin asked.

"Perhaps," the man said, shaking his head with a bitter smile. "I thought I was invisible, until you started speaking to me."

Kevin's eyes widened. *Invisible!*

With his heart beating wildly, Kevin asked the man if it was true; had he mastered such an ability and begged to learn how he had done it. The man looked at him carefully, before sinking down onto his heels. After a moment, he began to tell a story, one Kevin could hardly believe. Apparently, the man had always wanted to go unseen; to disappear, just like Kevin longed to do. One night, he'd been walking through a forest when a spirit appeared and told him he could grant his wish. The catch was as follows: the only way the man could ever become visible again would be if he found someone who desired invisibility just like he had.

When Kevin expressed his immense desire to assume the gift, the man's eyes narrowed.

"Are you sure?"
Kevin assured him he was.

The man told Kevin that he would have to take a journey to a place called "The Healing

Forest." It sounded strange, and Kevin wondered if it might be some trick.

"Where can I find this place?" he whispered.

The man gave him directions and told him that on his journey through the woods he would meet the people who would assist him in achieving his goal.

Anxious, Kevin asked for their names and descriptions; but the man said there was no need for such details.

"You will find out everything soon enough."

His heart beat hard in his chest as Kevin realized an amazing opportunity had been laid before him—if he had the strength to take it. As it was early in the day, he decided to leave right away for the forest, and try to make it home by curfew.

After walking for hours, Kevin finally spotted the tops of the trees. As he walked into the shadows underneath the branches, he began to doubt his decision. He stopped and turned as if to retreat to his school, but his desire to become invisible overrode his fears.

As he took one bold step after another, he noticed the odd shapes of the towering trees and strange animal noises. The canopy blocked out most of the sunlight, and the air stood still. It was intimidating, but it also sparked Kevin's curiosity. He wondered how such a spooky place could be called a "healing forest." A squirrel darted past as if it didn't have a care in the world. The creature was comfortable in its home, happy just being alive.

If only I could feel the same for a single moment.

The boy had been walking for some time when he felt a strange presence behind him. His thoughts raced as he remembered the stranger's words: "*Certain people will join you on your journey.*"

"Hello, is anyone there?" He hated how his voice trembled, but it couldn't be helped.

Looking over his shoulder, Kevin noticed a large shadow moving through the trees. It seemed too big to be human. He waited, frozen with fear, until the shadow got closer, revealing a giant man with a disfigured face. His clothing was tattered and well-worn.

Afraid, Kevin squeaked, "What is your name?"

The man responded, but his voice was so deep and gravelly Kevin could hardly hear what he said. Keven moved closer.

"I can't hear you Sir. Are you here to help me?"

The giant crouched and his gruesome face hovered close to Kevin's.

"My name is Shame, and I am here to help you become invisible."

Kevin wondered how such a formidable figure could speak so quietly. He tried to ask

Shame some questions about the forest, but the man looked away each time Kevin tried to address him.

Despite Shame's terrible appearance, Kevin felt comfortable around him, like he was an old friend. The two continued walking, as Shame escorted Kevin deeper into the woods.

They had only gone a short distance when Shame's huge, plodding feet suddenly stopped. Shame covered Kevin and told him not to move. As they stood still, Kevin heard the brushing of tree branches in the gloom ahead and squeezed his eyes shut in fear. The noise got louder, and he felt Shame stand up.

"Relax," he murmured. "It's just an old friend."

Kevin opened his eyes and noticed a stocky man standing before them.

"Kevin, this is Fear," said Shame.

Their new companion was short, only slightly taller than Kevin, but he had extremely large muscles. Just to look upon him was intimidating. Chains and locks hung loosely around his neck. Just as Kevin was about to ask him why he was wearing such heavy, ugly things, Fear threw them around Kevin's hands and feet. The boy cried out in surprise, but Fear assured him that the chains were only there to restrict Kevin's movement, and protect him while he was in the forest. Fear advised Kevin not to go anywhere without him. The rule was set: Fear would go before Kevin and survey the path, then return to tell Kevin of all the dangerous things awaiting him. Fear's job was to prevent Kevin from changing his mind about becoming *invisible*.

After listening to Fear, Kevin wondered if he had done the right thing by entering the forest. *Do I really want to be invisible so badly?* Just as he was pondering his decision, a loud roar thundered through the still air.

"What was that?" Kevin asked.

"Oh, that's just Anger," responded Fear. "Be careful around him, as he's got a short fuse."

To Kevin's disappointment, Shame and Fear began walking toward the noise. They soon reached an opening in the trees, which revealed a small, active volcano. Sitting amid the rocks and magma was a boy about Kevin's age.

"Did he make that loud noise all by himself?" Kevin asked.

"Shh…" Fear whispered. "Don't let appearances fool you. When he gets angry, he's capable of destroying everything around him."

The little boy's dark eyes flickered towards the three of them standing in the shadows. *He looks angry*, thought Kevin.

"Hello Anger, what are you doing?" Shame smiled meekly.

"What does it look like I'm doing?" the boy snapped back. "And who is that scrawny little runt beside you?"

His eyes narrowed in annoyance, and the air around Kevin seemed to grow hotter.

"Fear, can you give the kid some breathing room? It's enough that Shame is smothering him."

Kevin's two new friends shifted obediently, and Kevin felt a slight weight lift from his shoulders that he hadn't even realized was there.

"My name is Kevin," he said softly. "We heard your roar. Are you upset?"

"Upset?" He made a short, sharp bark of a laugh. "I'm in a dark forest, sentenced to a lifetime of stirring hot lava. *Why wouldn't I be upset?*" His sooty hands stretched wide across the hellish scene, and Kevin wondered why he didn't just walk away from it all. No one was keeping him here.

"Where did you find this brilliant kid?" Anger continued. "Under a rock?"

"We didn't find him—he found us," Fear stammered.

"So where is that other loser who hangs out with you knuckleheads? What's his name again?"

Fear's dark eyes sparkled in amusement.
"Guilty! I've never seen such a nosey idiot."

Kevin noticed movement across the clearing, and a moment later Anger Stood up and pointed, "There he goes!" They followed Anger's directions to the top of a mulberry tree, where a man was cowering in the branches.

"Why is he hiding in a tree?" Kevin asked.
"Tell him Guilt," crowed Anger. "Tell him how you hide, hoping to catch someone doing something wrong." The lava around Anger began to bubble and spit as the small boy

stood with his hands clenched into fists and stared up at the tree.

"Tell him how you and Shame team up to make people feel small. I bet you've been whispering secrets in his ear about disappearing, haven't you? But tell him the truth." Anger's eyes shot sparks, and the ground beneath their feet rumbled.

"You love nothing more than making a big man feel small and pushing souls into corners until they can't help but explode," Anger continued.

"Calm down!" cried Fear.

"Shut up you pathetic coward!" A small avalanche of rocks rolled down the volcano scattering at their feet. Kevin longed to run back into the forest, but Fear and Shame blocked his path. "You're just afraid to tell the truth because you know you can't survive in this freaking place without Shame and Guilt keeping you company!"

As Anger roared at them, he grew larger and turned bright red. His muscles bulged out of his clothing, and steam began to spew from the volcano behind them.

Fear leaned down to Kevin and whispered, "Anger is never happy around Shame and Guilt. He says Guilt always hides behind Shame, and he thinks they both team up on him to make him feel insignificant."

After Anger calmed down, Kevin sat by his side. The two discussed Kevin's life and the many things in it that made him angry. In no time, Anger became the boy's most dependable friend. Whenever Shame and Fear began to crowd him, Anger fended them off. He was very good at pushing people away and always knew exactly what Kevin wanted.

In the afternoon, Kevin and Anger walked up to the lip of the volcano. Rocks and sticks, spiders, and stinging ants...anything they did not like was tossed into the magma. Kevin felt bold and courageous. Anger might have been lonely at times, but no one messed with him like they messed with Kevin. Having said that, Kevin did not always like Anger's attitude as he was disrespectful and often hard to control.

Eventually, Guilt emerged from the tree, and Kevin saw that he wore a judge's robe and carried a gavel. His eyes were very large and seemed to see right through Kevin's soul.

Looking at Guilt made Kevin feel dirty, like something was wrong with him. Whenever the large eyes gazed upon him, Kevin would quickly look away.

As the small group of friends moved through the trees, Kevin reminisced about leaving the forest for a better life. *Perhaps I don't need to be invisible after all. Maybe I could rejoin the world and seek out those who felt fear and shame, or anger and guilt. I could soothe their pain and see if I could make them feel better.*

When Kevin voiced this idea, Guilt quickly convinced him that he was wrong for wanting to be visible in the world. With a somber expression, Guilt explained that wanting to feel good was selfish. Kevin relented and continued through the forest until a strange smell stopped him.

"Phew! What is that?"

Fear started to say something only to stop and point above their heads. Nestled in the branches was a very dark figure with sharp teeth and small, piercing eyes. His awful countenance was not helped by his repulsive odor, a mix of something like rotten meat and curdled blood; which made Kevin sick to his stomach. Kevin did not know this figure, but he didn't like the way the creature made him feel.

When he asked the figure for a name, he refused to tell him, but eventually Shame whispered, "Pain."

"Pain?"

Kevin did not like Pain, so as they continued along their path, he ignored him as much as possible.

Walking along, Kevin noticed that he and his friends always settled into a familiar formation. Shame would walk up front, with Guilt at the rear. Fear and Anger were on Kevin's left and right, keeping him boxed in. As they continued, Kevin's shadow slowly began to disappear, and an hour or so later, he realized he had finally become invisible! Now nothing in the forest could hurt him, and his new friends kept him from deviating from the path. Kevin felt wonderful; no more bullies or bad men lurking under the bleachers; no more grumbling mother; and no grumpy brother. Kevin was safe at last.

The new friends were deep inside the healing forest when Kevin glimpsed a new figure moving rapidly through the shadows. He had been following them for some time. Kevin didn't mention this to the others, who seemed not to notice.

That night, they settled around a campfire to reminisce about all the bad things Kevin had experienced in his life. Just as Kevin was talking about how Kenny liked to flush his head in the school's toilets, Kevin noticed the strange figure hovering in the moonlight. To his surprise, it was a beautiful woman with bronze skin. Her jet-black hair blew in the wind, and while she seemed as light as a ghost, there was a stillness about her that promised great strength.

Kevin stuttered to a stop, with his eyes fixed upon the mysterious apparition. She seemed to be pulling on his spirit and calling for him to join her. Energy tingled through his body, and for the first time, Kevin realized how tired and empty he felt. He looked around the campfire and saw that his friends had continued talking without him. No one had noticed the beautiful woman. Perhaps he was dreaming…the forest plays strange tricks on the mind.

"You can't see her?" Kevin said, interrupting Guilt as he argued with Anger about eating too much of their dinner.

"See who?" asked Fear, his eyes darting around.

"The lady over there with bright eyes."

Without waiting, Fear, Guilt, and Shame quickly ran behind some rocks and hid. Anger stood up and told Kevin he must never mention the lady again or go toward her.

"But who is she?"

"Trouble." Anger stomped out the ashes of their fire and collected their things. In stony silence, they continued their journey deeper into the woods.

As they trudged through the undergrowth, Kevin's thoughts lingered on his family. For all their grumbling, he missed them a lot. He'd give anything to sit in his mother's kitchen one more time. He might even eat at the table instead of in his room.

Every time he had a positive thought, he'd see the female figure gliding through the trees. Though he wasn't meant to watch her, he found he couldn't help himself. As his friends kept walking, a soft wind rustled through the leaves. The voice was silvery and full of light. She whispered that her name was Hope. Kevin asked her why she had to hide so much, and she responded that she was always there, he just couldn't see her.

Hope told Kevin she could help him escape the healing forest, but he would have to leave his friends behind. The thought made his heart clench in fear and his stomach curl with guilt. Leaving his friends would make him feel ashamed, and the fact that she made such a cruel demand left him prickling with anger. After all, they had helped him traverse the darkness, so how could he just forget about them?

Hope explained that his friends wanted to keep him in the forest forever and thereby keep him from the true path of healing.

"The true path?"

"Yes, Kevin. To be *visible* to the world, rather than hide away from it."

But Hope would not force him to walk from the darkness out into the light because he had to follow voluntarily. Kevin's ability to see her was his first step to finding his freedom. Despite being surrounded by negative influences, Kevin saw her because deep down, he desired to know himself better.

"If you hate the forest so much," Kevin asked, "why do you live here?"

"People can't see me in the light," Hope answered. "I can only be found in dark and difficult places where souls really need me."

Kevin nodded, his mind filling with contentment and peace. The sense of safety he had felt before was nowhere near as comforting as how Hope made him feel now. It was the difference between surviving and living.

"I wish I had found you sooner." he smiled. "There must be many souls out there who need you."

"I am sure you will find a way to tell them about me."

Kevin frowned. "People don't tend to listen to me."

"That was because you were invisible, before. You must be brave. People like you must tell the world I exist. You must be willing to face your pain in order to find happiness."

"You make it sound easy."
Her crystal eyes were so intent that Kevin's fears began to melt away.

"Your mind is challenging you, but you must listen to your heart. It wants you to be loved, valued, and celebrated. Your mind only seeks invisibility. It wasn't your mind that guided you to me, but your heart," she told Kevin. "Our hearts are what make us visible to the world."

Kevin sighed, sensing the truth in her words, but unable to truly trust them.

"You see, Kevin, whenever your pain is buried, so is your treasure. You wanted to become invisible and bury your pain; but you were also burying your greatest treasure, your true self."

As Hope put her arm around Kevin, the snap of a twig stopped her. Startled, Kevin looked back and saw Fear hiding behind a large oak tree. He had been following them but seemed too afraid to come any closer.

"Should we just run away?" Kevin whispered.

"No," Hope replied. "You can't escape Fear by simply avoiding him. You must face him."

Kevin took a deep breath. "We can see you Fear."

With a trembling voice, Fear replied, "You must choose Kevin. You cannot become friends with Hope and live with us."

Fear reminded Kevin how dangerous it was living outside the forest, and of the terrible things he had experienced there. Fear was very good at describing danger, and Kevin felt his body prickle with concern as different memories returned. As Fear talked, the chains and locks his friend had placed around his limbs felt heavier.

As they were talking, Kevin noticed that Guilt was sitting in the tree above them, listening to their conversation. With his face twisted into a scowl, he asked how Kevin could just turn his back on all his friends after everything they had done for him.

"We miss you," said Guilt, his face growing softer.

As Guilt continued talking, Kevin felt the positive energy inside his chest melt away, leaving him feeling empty once more. With a sigh, he agreed to return to the camp. He didn't like being in the middle of so much conflict, as he only wanted everyone to be happy. Hope seemed disappointed with his decision but didn't criticize his choice. Instead, she made him promise to return and see her the next morning.

During the days that followed, Kevin mostly sat around the camp with his friends, stealing away into the woods only at sunrise to speak with Hope. One morning as the sky began to grow lighter, Shame watched Kevin pack his bags. He knew his friend was going to meet Hope and had often noticed that the boy returned from their little meetings in a positive mood and refused to give any of them any attention.

Shame tried to talk Kevin out of leaving them, and when the boy ignored him, he clung to him closely, refusing to let him go. Kevin had to pry Shame off him, and sometimes the struggle left Kevin so exhausted that he gave up on his plan and slept instead.

The next time Kevin went to visit Hope, he found her surrounded by four other women. Sitting together in the early sunlight, they were laughing and looked so comfortable together they could have been sisters.

"I want you to meet my friends Joy, Compassion, Love, and Forgiveness," Hope said.

When Kevin returned to the campsite later that morning, he knew it was time to bid farewell to his friends. As he approached Fear, he noticed another person sitting beside him, Pain. The awful creature still smelled terrible, but Kevin was surprised that for the first time since meeting him, he addressed Pain directly instead of ignoring him. His time with Hope had made him stronger.

Anxiety pulsed through Kevin's heart as he assembled his old friends to say a final farewell.

"Shame, Fear, Guilt, Anger, and Pain, it is time for us to part ways."

This announcement released a tidal wave of complaints, threats, and pleading. Normally, Kevin would have found this overwhelming, but instead, he raised his hands and subdued their voices into silence.

"I know that in your own way, you have tried to protect me, and I thank you for that."

He peered into their eyes and saw their grudging understanding.

"And I know you will always be a part of my life."

This seemed to make them a little happier, though in truth, Kevin knew he'd rather leave them behind forever. To live in the light, a person must occasionally encounter darkness.

"But," he added, "I have new friends now."

At that moment, Hope, Joy, Compassion, Love, and Forgiveness appeared at the edge of the forest, their arms open in welcome.

"Are you ready to meet the world, Kevin?" asked Hope.

"No, he's not!" shouted Fear.

"He shouldn't!" said Guilt.

"He can't!" cried Shame.

"Yes," said Kevin. He waved goodbye to his friends and walking forward.

Part II—Kevin Leaves the Forest

"Kevin...KEVIN!"

Kevin was yanked back into reality as the flight attendant asked to see his plane ticket. He was daydreaming and second-guessing himself about leaving home for the first time. He was holding up the line and people were getting frustrated with him. That is when a guy pulled him by the arm and said, "Come on kid, get your head out the clouds! Hope told me I would need to force you onto the plane."

Wait! You know Hope?"

"Yes, I do. Now shut up, and let's get you on this plane."

Kevin followed the stranger to the back of the plane where they placed their baggage in the overhead compartment.

Kevin told the stranger, "You can have the window seat. I am not a big fan of flying."

As Kevin sat in his seat next to the stranger, his mind began to wander. He thought about his past, and how far he had come. He began to think how much he would miss his family, and the time he spent in the Healing Forest. Kevin was a different person now, and he wanted to find out what the world had to offer him.

Soon after leaving the Healing Forest, Kevin spent a lot of time with Hope. She told him that he would have to leave home and seek out his purpose if he was ever going to be happy. Hope also told Kevin he had to let go of what he had grown accustomed to in life. This made him sad as Kevin had structured his life around what made him feel safe. He loved listening to Hope's advice, but she told him again that it was time to leave. The plane lifting off the runway jolted Kevin from his thoughts.

Emerging from his deep thoughts and looking at the stranger next to him, Kevin asked, "What is your name?"

"My name is Courage, and I have been sent to help you take the next step in your journey on becoming visible to the world."

Kevin responded, "But I thought leaving the healing forest was the only thing I needed to do in order to become comfortable being in the world."

"No Kevin, leaving the forest was only the beginning. You needed to meet Hope to get out of the dark forest. The forest was keeping you from the next part of your journey. You will need me to make it through the next phase of your journey, self-discovery."

"Self-discovery?"

"Yes Kevin, I am here to help you find what you are seeking. Overcoming Fear, leaving Shame, getting rid of Guilt, and facing Pain was only the start. Now the real work begins."

As they settled into their seats, Kevin asked, "But why do I need to know you?

Courage responded, "Frankly, without me, you cannot do anything."

"Really? I was always told that all I needed was faith to be successful."

Laughing, Courage assured Kevin he had a lot to learn. "Kevin, we were all born to fulfill a purpose. However, most people never discover why they were born because they think it comes automatically. The moment we are born we are shaped by our social environments. Sometimes this robs us of our true potential."

"Geesh! Being visible is a lot of work."

Laughing still, Courage responded, "Yes, it is Kevin. That's why many people choose to remain hidden."

Courage asked Kevin, "So what were you daydreaming about anyway back there at the terminal?"

"Oh, I remember before my friend Hope left, she said that if I wanted to become happy in the world that I would have to become a seeker. Do you know what she meant by that, Courage?

"No, I do not, but to answer your question about faith; people prefer to use faith as a buzzword because it requires little action on their part. Real faith is when you act out what you believe and that takes knowing me, Courage. For instance, your faith brought you the airport, but it took me, Courage, to get you on the plane. Did you look at your ticket and notice it does not have a destination?"

Kevin looked at his ticket and noticed it was a one-way ticket to nowhere. He became angry and asked, "Why would Hope send me to a place I have never been before?"

"Kevin, Hope knew you would never leave if she told you the truth."

"What truth?"

"Success comes from taking risks. You see, Kevin, most people are unwilling to leave their security and venture into unknown territory. However, in order to grow, you must let go of your security and the familiar things in your life. These things often stifle your growth and keep you enslaved."

Kevin knew Courage was telling him the truth, but he did not like the way it made him feel.

While Kevin was having a conversation with Courage on the plane, he noticed an older man staring at him. The man seemed familiar. It was like Kevin had seen him before. If Kevin did not know any better, he could have sworn it was the same man who told him about the "Healing Forest." This was the first time Kevin saw the man in the light. He noticed the man had some of his same features. The man reminded Kevin of himself.

As Kevin stared at him, Courage interrupted and asked, "Does that guy make you feel uncomfortable?"

"A little bit. Do you know who he is?" asked Kevin.

"The man staring at you is the same man who directed you to the Healing Forest," explained Courage.

"I knew he looked familiar. But he looks much better. He appears to have gotten better since he left the dark space beneath the bleachers. How do you know him, Courage?"

"Kevin, that is your future self. The better you become in the present, the better and more you will improve your future looks. In fact, Kevin, you created him."

"I created him?"

"Yes, He has been with you the whole time. He is a part of you. Don't worry as in time, you two will join and become one."

The plane began to descend to its destination.

Kevin looked at Courage and asked, "where are we landing?"

"We are going to a strange land that you have never seen or experienced. Kevin, it is here that you will learn more about yourself than you have before. Nothing here will be familiar to you. The first person you will encounter in this new place will be Failure."

"Failure?" Kevin asked.

"Yes! Failure will be your guide and teacher on the first part of your journey. You must get along well with Failure before you can be introduced to the next phase of your journey.

As Courage was talking to Kevin, he began to reminisce and recall how much he missed his friends in the forest.

"What are you daydreaming about now?" asked Courage.

"Oh, nothing!"

"Get your head out the clouds young man and focus on what lies ahead. We are about to land.

The plane landed and taxied to the gate. Kevin looked out the window and noticed they were surrounded by nothing but desert.

"Where are we?"

"The wilderness," responded Courage. "We are in the wilderness."

Kevin asked, "Why in the world would I want to leave the dark depressing forest just to come to the freaking wilderness?"

"It is in the place of nothingness that you discover the treasure you carry within you."

Kevin looked at his body and thought to himself, *Treasure within me?*

As Kevin and Courage exited the plane, the sweltering heat beat against Kevin's face. Courage walked confidently in front of him, leaving him lagging behind. He seemed to be walking away from the airport terminal into the hot desert.

Kevin yelled, "Where are you going? The airport is this way."

"There is nothing in there we need!" Courage shouted back.

"What about our bags?" pleaded Kevin.
"You won't need them out here."

Courage continued, "Remember Kevin, you have to let go of things you are accustomed to and the luxuries of your past. They will only imprison you and cause you to remain stuck. You can always stay at the airport if your only concern is security. You don't need me in secure places. I only live in the unknown and unpredictable places in your life. You cannot be my friend and remain in familiar places. That's why few people know me by my real name.

"Most people prefer to know me as Faith. Calling me Faith allows people to dream about being happy but getting to know me as Courage causes them to act. Very few people with faith act out what they believe. They think simply believing is enough to get by in life. The Creator of the Universe can never use such people. History shows that everyone the Creator used to effect change had to be acquainted with me personally, Courage.

"Kevin, you cannot live by faith alone. You need me, Courage, to make a difference in the world. You must know me by my God-given name, Courage. Believing is not enough. The proof that you believe something is that you have the courage to do it. So, are you going to just stand there looking stupid or are you going to join me?"

Kevin looked back at the airport terminal. He saw that most of the people filing into the double doors. He wanted to join the others so badly, but knew if he was to discover his purpose, he needed Courage. Kevin put his head down and ran to catch up with Courage; and the two began the long walk to what seemed like nowhere.

After walking most of the day, they came to a small town. Kevin's clothing was torn and soaked with perspiration. He was extremely thirsty, and his stomach ached from hunger.

Remembering that he left all his clothing and money back at the airport, Kevin thought to himself, *why in the world did I allow Courage to talk me into this?* Kevin now wished he had listened to his logic.

They entered a new town in the middle of the day. All Kevin could think of was getting something to eat. The people in the new town seemed busy and going their own way. Kevin was too embarrassed to ask for help. He asked Courage how they would survive in a town where no one knew their names.

Courage reminded him, "I am only here to assist you Kevin, and you must make the decisions."

"I will get a job," responded Kevin.

Courage responded, "I knew you would say that. Most people think money and a job are the answers to their problems. People spend most of their lives working jobs to survive and live their whole life to survive. People want security instead of freedom. They never discover why they were born. They have brief moments of happiness, but most of their lives are spent toiling for the bare necessities of life. They complain about what they don't have and admire the happiness enjoyed by the few people who live out their purpose."

Shaking his head, Courage continued, "These same people love to be entertained and spend frivolously on mundane things. All

of their motivation comes from external things they believe can bring them happiness. They are wasters of time and see little value in the simple things in life. They are afraid to be different and will do anything to fit in with the majority. They are willing to risk it all to gain the world but lose their soul in the process. So, if that is what you desire Kevin, then yes, getting a job is a great idea. But remember, you could have survived in the forest if survival was your only goal. You left the forest to thrive and live the life you were created to live."

Kevin argued, "So if I don't get a job, how can I...?

Courage interrupt him, "...survive?"
"What will I do?"

"Kevin take a look around, see how you can contribute to the people around you. Your life is not only about you, but what you contribute to the world. What have you learned on your journey so far that can benefit the people of this town?"

Kevin got settled in his room and began thinking about all the things Courage said to him. He thought, *What's wrong with a job? Everybody I know have jobs and they seem to be happy.* Just then Kevin remembered how his family and friends often complained about their jobs.

He began to get depressed until he remembered Hope telling him he had a gift. She told him that he had to find a way to use his gift. She told him that it would be something that he was naturally good at. Kevin tried to figure out what he was good at doing. He also remembered Hope told him that his gift was meant to solve a problem. The two would go together like a puzzle. The problem would also be something that bothered him.

Kevin slowly got up from his bed and looked out the window and noticed how the people walking by seemed so sad. This made him even more depressed. *Why does people's sadness bother me?* It was then he remembered how he liked to cheer people up and always dreamed of helping people become successful. He would always give his brothers pep talks; and took great pride in encouraging the kids in the neighborhood. *Ah ha, that's it! My gift is to encourage people.*

Kevin readily began his dream of trying to encourage the people of the dry, boring town located in the middle of the desert. He would go into town in the morning and watch the people as they began their day. He noticed how the people walked around with sullen faces. Everyone seemed to be in a hurry and were very busy. Kevin noticed how the parks were empty and there were no sounds of children playing. Everyone kept to themselves and the people made very little eye contact with each other. The people seemed like the walking dead.

Kevin went up to people and attempted to say hello, but all he got were strange stares. No one even seemed to notice he was alive. *This is no use*, he thought to himself. *What now?*

Courage reminded him that he had to make the decisions. Courage asked, "What problem do you see with the people in the town?"

"The people seem…well…."

Courage interrupted, "Invisible?"

"Yes, that's the word I was looking for."

"And since you know what that feels like Kevin, maybe you can help the people in this town become more visible and see life the way you now see it."

Kevin's eyes got big and his heart raced as he began to feel like he could help others overcome what he endured.

Late that night, Kevin sat on his bed and began to plan how he would help people overcome their fears. A knock at the door snatched Kevin from his daydreaming. He opened the front door and saw Hope.

Surprised Kevin asked, "How did you get here?"

"Remember Kevin that I show up in the most difficult places. But, as I told you, many cannot see me because of their mindsets."

Kevin had not seen Hope since he left the Healing Forest.

I see you are having a hard time in this new place. Did you ever wonder why I would send you to such a distant place on your own?"

"Yes," Kevin replied. "I was angry with you. Why would you send me here knowing that I would get discouraged?"

"Well Kevin, it was the only way you would discover your treasure."

Kevin began each day speaking great things to people in the attempt to get them to come hear him speak of life's greatest treasures. But the people walked past him as if he didn't exist.

After months of trying to encourage others, Kevin became even more discouraged. He would drag himself out of bed each morning. He hated the long, hot days that waited on him as he exited his small tent. Thoughts assaulted his mind about home. He wished he had just remained with his family, gotten a job, and settled down in his hometown. But something within Kevin told him that living that type of life would not have made him happy.

Courage visited Kevin and began to explain. "You see Kevin, everything we experience in life has meaning and can be used to make the world better. However, if we never allow ourselves to feel and let life ask the deep question our hearts seek, we will always feel lost. Our lives speak a language only we can understand."

Kevin felt utterly useless. He left his small room and found Courage.

"Courage, I am leaving."
"Where will you go?" asked Courage.
"I do not know. Things are really hard right now and I am not fit to be alive. I can't even

encourage myself, so how can I encourage others?"

Courage responded, "Well Kevin, you cannot run away each time you have a setback and things do not go your way."

"The people here do not appreciate my presence and what I have to offer. I will go somewhere and find people that like me."

"Kevin, is this about the people, or is this about you and how you honestly feel about yourself?"

"What do you mean?"

"It sounds to me like you are having some internal struggles about your ability. The value of your gift is not determined by other people, it is determined by you. You can go ahead and leave, but remember, I found you the first time. If you leave this time, you will find it difficult to locate me again."

Kevin laughed and said, "Well, you should be easy to find in this small town."

"You have never had to look for me Kevin, I am very difficult to find in hard times."

"Whatever. I can make it on my own," Kevin replied.

"Growth begins with separation. However, many people think the more they gain, the more successful they become. It is not what you gain, but what you are able to give that determines your happiness. This calls for resistance. Kevin, the creator of the world incorporated resistance in the creative process. This means that we need resistance to cause our creativity to manifest itself. You are like most people who want to take the least path of resistance. As a result, we never discover our creative selves. Nothing is created without resistance. Kevin you are waiting for validation and permission from other people. This type of mindset will only imprison you. You appear to be looking for something, but what you are looking for is inside of you."

As they were walking through the town, Kevin saw a man yelling in the middle of the street. No one was listening to him.

Kevin jokingly asked Courage, "Is that the town's clown?"

"No Kevin!" replied Courage. "That is the guy I was telling you about. His name is Failure. Some people refer to him as Wisdom."

"Why are people ignoring him?"

"Most people don't like Failure because of how he makes them feel. However, Failure is an excellent teacher. In fact, no one can be successful without first being mentored by Failure. He is one of the persons you must get to know if you are to learn why you exist."

Courage pointed in the opposite direction. Kevin turned to see a large crowd of people growing more anxious by the minute about something.

"What are they doing?" Courage stated, "Let's go find out."

As they got closer, Kevin noticed the long lines and the people's excitement. He thought, *Wow, maybe someone famous may be giving a speech or putting on an act.*

But when they got closer, Kevin could not believe his eyes. The people were all gathered around a large female statue surrounded by a deep pond of water. The statue had large jewels embedded throughout its structure. As Kevin looked even closer, he noticed people tossing money and valuables at the statue.

"Why are they throwing money and valuables at her?" Kevin asked.

Courage responded, "Kevin, that is Lady Luck. There is a story that says if you give lady luck your attention and your valuables, she will one day return the favor by blessing you with good fortune. So everyday people come and worship her, hoping she will change their fate."

"Have you ever witnessed her bless anyone with good fortune?"

"Yes, but it rarely occurs; and for the few that she does bless, there is a rumor that she also destroys. Many say her rewards also come with curses. So, tell me who would you rather give your attention to?"

Kevin stated, "I would rather deal with failure than depend on luck. At least Failure is someone I can talk to and ask for direction, whereas Lady Luck just seems to be a tale."

"Are you sure? I must warn you that when you begin dealing with Failure, you will have to make some difficult decisions. You will discover things about yourself you never knew. I will introduce you to him."

Failure pointed toward a tent, "Look, you see the large elephant over there tied to the stake? He wants to leave and go join his family in the wild, but he cannot."

"What is stopping him? It is obvious no one in the town can stop him."

"You answered correctly. In fact, no one is trying to stop him. He remains in place because he spent years with Fear. Have you met Fear?"

"Yes, I have."

"Fear was introduced to the elephant at a very young age. He embraced Fear and never released him. You see how we learn by making mistakes, yet people are afraid of making mistakes and this keeps them from learning. That is why people avoid me. They think I will cause them hardship, but in reality, it is I, Failure, who helps people find their way. When people don't encounter me, they follow the paths of others and never discover their own way."

Kevin asked Failure, "Do you know where I can find Courage?"

"I know one thing is certain; you will never find Courage by asking other people. You must follow your heart. However, there is one person who may be able to assist you."

Kevin looked up and for the first time since being with Failure, he stared Failure directly in the face. He asked, "Where can I find this person, and what is their name?"

"You don't find this person, as you have to be led to her."

"Why is everything always so freaking hard to find around here?"

"That's exactly the point. You are looking for things that aren't lost. They are already within your grasp, but you cannot find them until you find yourself."

"Find myself? But I am not lost," stated Kevin sarcastically.

"Are you sure about that? You are searching for everyone, but yourself. Try finding yourself first, and the other things you are looking for will be easier to find. However, for now, the person that you must find in order to locate Courage is in that direction." And with that, Failure began to walk away.

"Wait! You told me she was a woman, but you never told me her name."

Failure responded, "Don't worry. You will know her the moment you two meet; but here is a formula that will make it easier: ask, seek, and knock."

Kevin waved goodbye to Failure, but he knew he would see him again. He reluctantly walked in the direction Failure pointed him.

Kevin found it difficult to find Courage while he was in his depressed mindset. Tired from his long journey, he decided to rest by a cactus near a small pond. The shade from the cactus gave him momentary refuge from the blistering heat. Awakened suddenly from a deep sleep by someone kicking his feet, Kevin looked into the sun in attempts to make out the shadowy figure that was hovering over him.

"Hi there, young fellow! What are you dreaming about?"

As Kevin shielded the sun from his eyes, he saw a middle-age man smiling from ear to ear.

"I wasn't dreaming, I was resting my eyes, that is until you interrupted me," Kevin said sarcastically.

The stranger responded, "My, my, aren't we in a sour mood to be so young!"

"Who are you and why do you have that stupid smile on your face?"

"Stupid smile? asked the stranger. "I smile because I am happy."

"Happy about what? What is there to be happy about in the middle of a freaking dessert?"

"Before I answer that question. Let me introduce myself. Hello, my name is Gratitude. There is a lot to be happy about, but you will never find out until you change your attitude."

Curious, Kevin asked, "What do you mean?"

Gratitude responded, "Everything we experience in life is meant to teach us a valuable lesson about why we were born. Life is not about living; it is about discovery. In fact, you are not who think you are! It is the label you have been given so other people can identify you. As long as you base your life on how other people identify you, you will never be happy. The goal in life is not to be successful, but to discover why you were born and sent into the world. Until you discover this, you will never be happy. You will become a wanderer of the earth, forever searching for something that does not exist."

"Decisions are often forced upon us while choices are made within us. This is where attitude comes into the picture. We cannot always control what happens to us, but we can always control how we respond."

Gratitude embraced Kevin and told him it was time for them to part ways. Kevin began to get sad, but Gratitude reminded him, "Growth begins with separation."

"But I thought you said that I should always keep you as a guide to see opportunities."

Before leaving, Gratitude gave Kevin an unmarked envelope. Kevin looked in the envelope and saw two seeds.

"What are these for?" he asked.

"Don't worry, you will need them later in your journey. You are to give them to the woman you will meet later in your journey."

"I heard you had a difficult time motivating people back in town."

Kevin frowned. "Yes, the people did not want to listen to anything I had to say."

"You mean they did not want to give you their attention?" questioned Gratitude.

"Yes, that is what I meant."
Gratitude laughed with his silly grin again.
"What's funny now?" Kevin asked.

"That is your problem. You are a taker and not a giver. You were trying to take from the people rather than give to them. You wanted them to give you their attention, time, money, affection, and possessions, but you were not willing to give them anything. Inspiration comes from giving not taking. You don't even like people, so how will you add value to them? The problem is not that you don't like people, you do not like yourself. You try to make others like you. Can't you see, your whole life has been shaped on what you can get from others and not what you can give. You will never be successful in life with that type of attitude."

"What attitude?" Kevin asked.

Gratitude told him that people don't see giving opportunities because of their attitudes. "I was sent to help give you the right attitude and change you from a taker to a giver. Have you ever heard the saying, "What a person sows, so shall they reap?"

"Yes, I have," said Kevin.

"Notice reaping only comes after sowing. Or put another way, receiving follows giving. Give what you want to receive. This is also true with your attitude. The universe gives you what you project onto it. If your attitude is that life is difficult, then that is how the universe reveals itself to you. It does not matter where you find yourself in life, if your attitude is right, you can change any situation into a positive one. In fact, your attitude gives people a sneak peek into your beliefs."

"My beliefs," questioned Kevin.

"Yes. We express what we believe through our attitudes. People who believe they have something to give to others often have a giving attitude. People who have a negative attitude often believe the world owes them something."

"Like I did back in town when I was speaking to the people?"

"Exactly! Having an attitude of gratitude also makes you a great listener. Instead of projecting onto the universe, you listen to its voice and the path it tries to lead you on."

Ask, Seek, Knock

As he walked, Kevin's mind wandered. *Find myself? I wonder what Failure meant by that. Why is everything worth having so hard to obtain? It seems like the things that matter the most don't come easy. I wish life were easier.*

If we were meant to live a life of purpose, why doesn't God just tell us what to do? Why would God conceal such an important aspect of our lives? I mean why did God allow me to suffer through the pain if he loved me so much? It is not fair for some people to enjoy life while many others suffer.

Happiness should be everyone's birthright not just the right of a few. Hmmm, maybe that's it, maybe we got happiness wrong. What if happiness does not come from doing things or accumulating riches? What if happiness comes from being our true selves?

Maybe that is the purpose of life—to discover why we were born. I wonder if I shift my focus from being successful to being happy if my journey to discovery will be easier. Then I might be able to motivate others to do the same thing because I have taken the journey myself and can talk about it convincingly.

Kevin was so caught up in his thoughts he was unaware of how far he had walked. Now he was a good-ways from the nearest town, and there was no one in sight. His lips were parched from the scorching heat. His body ached and he was dripping with sweat from the sun. Exhausted mentally and physically, Kevin could barely take another step. He couldn't turn around and go back as it was too far. He felt as if he would die of extreme thirst and hunger, yet he forged ahead in attempt to locate the nearest town.

After walking a little while longer, Kevin happened upon a well. As he drew closer to it, he noticed a woman sitting on top of it. With a gentleness that Kevin was not used to, the woman greeted him, "I see you found me. It was only because you were hungry and thirsty. If it had not been for this, you probably would have passed me by unnoticed. You see Kevin, most people find me like you did, when they are searching for something deeper than the world has to offer.

While around this intriguing woman known as Love, Kevin's senses were magnified. He began to see things from a new perspective. Instead of complaining about the sun's heat, he admired the sunrise and sunsets while in the desert. He observed the beauty of the town's people. He no longer complained about the long walks and took time to appreciate his breaths. Love made Kevin view life differently, and she made him radiate. Time even seemed to stand still when Kevin sought out and embraced Love.

As wonderful as it was to be around Love, at times, she also made Kevin feel very uncomfortable. He wanted to be around her, but he could not understand why his anxiety grew when she showed up. He asked Love about his ambivalent feelings, and she explained that his feelings came from his concern about loss and death.

"Tell me about your meeting with Failure. What did you learn from him?"

"The first thing he told me was to learn to listen to him."

"That is right. Most people do not listen to Failure. They just see him coming and go the other way to avoid him. But, if they would have stopped to listen to him, he would have introduced them to his best friend, Success. Most people never get to meet Success because they are too afraid of Failure."

With worry written all over his face and a waiver in his voice, Kevin confided to Love that Failure never introduced him to Success.

Love laughed, "I didn't say he would introduce you to Success. Success will never come looking for you. You must use the advice Failure gave you to find Success."

"Why am I always the one looking for the people who can help me?"

"Because you are seeking to find yourself, you cannot remain where you are to find yourself. One of the hardest lessons you will learn on the road to happiness is that the same people that got you where you are cannot carry you where you need to go. That is why letting go is so significant in this part of your journey. The illusion of security is what keeps many people trapped in their current lives."

"So why are you telling me this and why now?"

"You cannot accept this truth without me, Love. Neither Courage, Failure nor Hope could have revealed this truth to you. Most people discover this truth when they encounter me but choose to ignore it. You will be faced with the same decision."

"What decision is that?"

"Have you ever heard of demons?"
"Yes, I have!" exclaimed Kevin wide eyed.

"Some of the Sages believe that demons are trapped souls. And if they stay trapped too long, they become destructive, first against themselves then against others. Out in this wilderness is where many people realize they are trapped souls. It is also in the wilderness that individuals are given the opportunity to stay trapped or to be released and become a free spirit. This is what you are experiencing in the wilderness. Just like in the forest you have an important decision to make, be free or remain trapped."

Almost as if Love were reading Kevin's mind, she asked, "Do I make you uncomfortable?"

"Yes. Why do I feel this way around you? People always told me that once I found you that my life would become easier."

Love smiled at Kevin as she moved closer to him. "This is the misperception many people have about me. This becomes their main motivation for finding me. It is not to become one with me but to use me to get what they want or to ease their pain. I do not work like that."

"As long as you are looking for me, it means that I reside outside of you. Until you can fully embrace me, you will always be looking for me. You cannot hold onto me. I was created to be shared, but many people want to control me. I live inside one's hearts."

"If you live outside of me, why am I able to see and talk to you?"

"You are talking to an allusion. You do what most people do when they want something bad enough; they create it. When people want something, they project it out into the world or onto someone else. In fact, the very thing they want already resides within their heart."

"This works for everything, including hatred. When you say you hate something or someone, it is because it is in your heart and you have objectified it so you can better control it. Love is about letting go not about obtaining something. When you love something or someone, you let go of the things that formerly mattered to you. This one fact keeps more people from embracing me than any other thing in the world. That is why I scare people."

"Deep down, they know to befriend me means they will have to let go of everything they have become so attached to. That is why you have been able to see me in the wilderness, the place of nothingness. You had to leave everything you were familiar with to come to this place. When there was nothing else outside of you to measure your value, you began looking inside."

"When you find me, Love, on the inside, then you are able to experience me in all things. People are not ready to embrace me until they are willing to let go of everything. Then and only then do I become significant to them."

"That is why the first thing the great teachers—Jesus, Buddha, and Muhammad—teach that you must be willing to let go and follow your heart. Many are afraid to follow their heart because of fear of losing control. If you can see me, you can control your interaction with me. But when I am in your heart, we become one and you cannot control me. You heard me correctly, you cannot control Love."

"Have you ever heard the story of Abraham from the Bible? He was constantly asked to let go of the things that mattered to him. People refer to this as sacrifice. The lesson here is that to truly love, you must learn to let go or sacrifice what matters most to you. Abraham had to let go of his family, his past, and his only begotten son. His son represented his image. That was the only way he could follow the path he was meant to live. You too must learn the lesson of letting go if you are ever going to find the path you were meant to live."

"But I left everything to discover my path," Kevin said emphatically.

"Are you sure about that? Perhaps you left some things, but you are still holding onto the thing that is most precious to you."

"And what is that?" asked Kevin.

"That is for you to figure out, but I will give you a small clue, it has something to do with your image. You are protecting an image that you have projected into the world. Know this; the moment you focus on gaining something, you lose everything."

"The fact that you can see me lets me know you are not ready to fully embrace me. It tells me that you are looking outside of yourself to find fulfillment. You see, I was created before the world came into existence."

Kevin's eyes widened, "Wow! You don't look that old to me!"

Love laughed. "That's because what you are looking at is a projection. I am what you want and desire. Like most people, you believe this is the only way to experience love. People often search for things or other people so they can experience love. In other words, most people are concerned with receiving love. The key to fulfillment is not receiving but giving. If you are going to be happy, you must look within and see what you have to offer the world. The reason you were unsuccessful in inspiring other people is because you wanted to receive adoration and love from the people. People intuitively sense when someone is taking from them. You are enough and do not need to receive anything. Your problem is, you don't know how to give."

Kevin asked Love what Hope meant when she said that *he would have to become a seeker in order to be happy.*

Love told Kevin, "There is a gift God planted inside of you. The only way to discover it is that you must seek it. Most people do what you do. They go searching for happiness outside of themselves when everything they need in life is within them. Have you ever heard the saying, 'What would it profit a man if he gains the world but loses his soul?'"

"Yes, I have."

"This is what this statement is referring to. Many people chase after worldly possessions and in the process, they forfeit their greatest gift, their authentic self. People spend their whole lives chasing after happiness when they possess the ability to be happy within."

"I understand that you were trying to motivate the people back in town; but do you know why you were unsuccessful?"

"No," replied Kevin.

"It is because you had not encountered yourself and had not yet embraced me as a part of you. Before you fall in love with a person or a thing, you must first fall in love with yourself. You cannot give what you do not possess."

Kevin's countenance grew sad because he never felt any love for himself. He had always searched for others to make him feel important.

Love continued, "Only then can you contribute to the world. What you have buried deep within you, is to be shared with the world. You must go out of your way to discover this gift and make it available to the world."

"But how do I discover this gift?"

"You learn to listen to your own voice. It will guide you. You have been trained to listen to others, but you have not learned to hear your own voice. What you are born to do must not feel like a task but a connection. Most people think that life will show them their purpose. This is not true. Some religious teachings tell people they are anointed for a task and have a purpose. This often makes people passive observers of their own lives. In order to discover your gift, you must seek it. You must first ask, 'Why am I here?' Then you must seek the answer to that question. When you don't get the answer, you must knock, or be persistent until you find why you were born. once you find the reason, you must then spend your life sharing your gift with the world."

"Most people say that I, Love, hurts. It is not that love hurts, it is the attempt to control love that hurts people. You see, seeking control is what keeps most people trapped and causes them pain. People want to control outcomes and other people, but this is not how the world was created."

"You were unsuccessful in the town when you tried to motivate them because you wanted to receive from the people, and not give to them. If you want to be successful you must be a contributor."

Kevin hung his head. Feeling defeated he asked, "Why is it so hard to find my purpose in life?"

"You never looked," responded Love. "Your whole life you have been doing what others suggested to you. You have been listening to others while your own voice remained silent."

Almost as if something had bit him, Kevin leaped to his feet as he remembered something Failure had told him. "Failure told me about a formula that would make it easier for me to find Courage. If I could only remember what he said. I believe it was ask, seek, and knock?"

"The first part of the formula is asking. You must ask yourself what it is you truly want out of life. Many people live their lives based on what other people suggest. Then once you ask the question you must seek out the answer with all your heart, with all your mind, and with all your soul. Obstacles will come up you, but that is when you must knock or be persistent until you discover your purpose in the world. Have you ever noticed that every great hero had to take a journey to find themselves before they could help other people? Kevin, your true spirit is buried beneath all the perceptions and beliefs others have given you."

Pausing, Kevin asked, "What do my beliefs have to do with my life?"

"Your beliefs control everything. Let me explain. Your eyes determine what you see, but your heart determines how you see."

"My heart?" asked Kevin with his hand on his chest.

"Yes, your heart and your beliefs determine how you see yourself, and how you see yourself determines how you see things around you. For instance, when you first met me, you were depressed and angry. You believed that if you left the place you were and relocated that you would be happier. You left but found yourself feeling the same way in the new location. That is because your beliefs never changed. Until you change what you believe, you will remain the same. In fact, you will recreate what you believe in every place you find yourself. Do you remember why you left home in the first place?"

"Actually, I do," Kevin responded. "I was unhappy!"

"You do what most do when they are unhappy; they attempt to change their situation while they themselves remain the same. You must work on changing yourself. You are transformed when you change the way you think. That only occurs when you face the true beliefs about yourself. There was something you were instructed to give me when you met me."

"Oh yeah, I had forgotten!" Kevin reached into his pocket and handed Love the two seeds Gratitude have given to him.

Love looked at the two seeds and shook her head.

Confused by this, Kevin asked, "What, do you not want them?"

"Do you not understand what the seeds represent?"

"No, but I am sure you are going to tell me."

Laughing Love asked Kevin, "What does a farmer do?"

"A farmer grows food," responded Kevin.

"Not exactly. A farmer creates an environment so food can grow. Seeds grow food, but they must be planted in the right environment. As powerful as the seeds are, they are useless unless planted in the right environment. As-long-as you hold onto the seeds, they have no power; but if you search for the right environment and plant the seeds, they will produce what they were meant to produce."

Confused Kevin asked, "But what do these seeds have to do with me?"

"The seeds represent one's potential. You must take great care to treat them with importance. Placing them in the wrong environment, the seeds will only remain buried. It is the responsibility of the seed holder to find the right environment for the seeds and nourish them until they produce what they were created for. Kevin, nothing grows is your pocket; not money, not ideas, not plans.

Kevin woke up the next morning eager to get to the location where he always found Love waiting for him. But when he arrived, he noticed that Love was not there. He panicked and began looking all over the field.

As he circled back around for a second time, he happened upon an old man. Kevin didn't remember seeing him before. The old man watched as Kevin paced back and forth.

Finally, the old man asked, "What are you looking for son?"

"I am looking for Love," Kevin responded shyly.

"Well, maybe I can help you."
The old man asked, "What does Love look like?"

Kevin tried to describe Love but noticed he could not think of a description. Puzzled he tried again, but no concise description came to mind.

Confused, the old man asked, "Do you know what Love looks like or not? You can't find Love if you do not know what she looks like son!"

Just as Kevin was about to say No, he remembered what Love taught him. *As-long-as he could describe Love, he was not ready to embrace her and become one with her. It is when you can no longer describe me in detail that you have come to embrace me, and I have entered your heart. I cannot be explained, Kevin. I can only be expressed.*

At that precise moment, Kevin's eyes were opened. It was then he realized that the old man was the same individual who introduced him to the Healing Forest. He walked over and embraced the old man, reached into his bag, and gave him his cloak.

"I won't be needing this anymore."

After that gesture, the old man turned around and began walking away. As Kevin watched, the old man disappeared into the distance.

As Kevin turned around to return to town, he noticed Courage standing right in front of him.

Surprised, Kevin asked, "I have been looking all over the place for you, where have you been?"

Courage responded, "I have been closer to you than you think."

"Why was it so hard to locate you?"

"Because you were trying to find me using fear and not with Love."

Part III—Kevin Stumbles Upon Passion

Kevin…KEVIN!

His shift manager startled Kevin as he stood at the cash register taking another customer's order.

"Step out of the way and go to the back and operate the dishwasher. I will have someone else help this customer."

The manager complained to the customer, "I apologize for that, ma'am. That young man is always daydreaming and just doesn't seem to know how to appreciate having a job. Young people these days."

Kevin slammed down his apron and went to the back to wash dishes. In a way, he was glad to be to himself. It gave him time to think. As he washed dishes, he couldn't help but think about his time in the Healing Forest and in the wilderness. It had been years since he heard from Hope, Courage, and Love. Why hadn't they contacted him? They promised they would visit, but Kevin wondered if he would ever see them again. He thought he had done all that was necessary to find his purpose and be happy. But deep inside, he knew something was missing. But what?

The workday couldn't end soon enough. As Kevin exited the restaurant, he looked over his shoulders and noticed his co-workers slaving over food and busting tables. As he walked away, sadness gripped his heart. His life sucked; he felt a sudden urge to quit. Kevin thought knowledge alone was enough to change his life. He had been taught a lot, but nothing had changed except his age.

It was Kevin's senior year of high school. He had succeeded in surviving the "reign of terror." After graduation, he moved out of his mother's home and found an apartment in the heart of the city. Working long hours and getting little sleep, he finally understood what his mom meant by, *"Money doesn't grow on trees!"* The saying made him again think of his time in the Healing Forest. The pain of his past was hard to forget. He just did not feel like he had what it took to be happy. He had spent time with Courage and remembered his teachings, *everything we experience in life has meaning and can be used to make the world better. However, if we never allow ourselves to feel and let life ask the deep question our hearts seek, we will always feel lost. Our lives speak a language only we can understand.* He only wished he had Courage with him at this very moment.

Kevin dreaded walking past the rundown neighborhood where he lived. He began to second guess his decision to leave the Healing Forest. He had not been in contact with Hope since she led him out of the forest. He wondered if he would ever see her again. It was getting late, and he didn't live in the safest neighborhood, he needed to get home. However, Kevin didn't want to be alone in his apartment with his thoughts. He needed some fresh air. A little walk wouldn't hurt.

Kevin decided to take the long way home, it would give him time to clear his head. Money was tight, and he was losing interest in his current job. Kevin wondered if he would spend his whole life working just to survive. He grew up watching his family struggle to make "ends meet." As his mind wandered, the sounds of the city drowned out his thoughts. For now, he needed to focus on making it home safely.

He passed a group of adolescent boys, who had made a game of harassing a homeless man in an alley. The man covered his head and began to scream for help. Kevin picked up his pace; he did not want the hoodlums to notice him. The man curled in the fetal position and looked in Kevin's direction.

Upon making eye contact with the man, Kevin felt a strong urge to help him. He stopped and turned toward the man. The kids noticed Kevin and started laughing. As he drew closer, the boys ran away.

Kevin approached the man and reached out his hand. "Are you okay, sir?"

Kevin attempted to help the man up, but he snatched away in fear.

"I am not going to hurt you."

Kevin noticed that the boys had dumped what little food the man owned, and they had poured hot coffee all over the tattered clothes he was wearing.

After realizing that Kevin was not part of the ill-mannered boys, the old man finally spoke. "It was nice of you to stop and help me young man, but I am okay." The man sat up and began to wipe the dirt from his face. "I...I...I will be okay. Thank you again."

Kevin noticed the man looking at his food sprawled all over the ground. He wished he had some money to give him.

Kevin asked the man where he lived. "Anywhere I can," he responded.

"What is your name?" Kevin asked.
"My name is not important."
"What is yours?"
"My name is Kevin. I work at the restaurant up the street."

"Mm, yes," the man smiled, "I know the place. It's where the heavenly smell of fresh apple pie hits my nose every morning. I tried eating there once, but I was run off by the manager."

"Oh, that's Craig. Don't mind him, he is mean to everyone. If you would like, I could bring you a piece of pie tomorrow on my way home from work."

"Yes son, that would be delightful. I will be right here. That is, if you can see me."

Kevin was confused. "What do you mean if I can see you?"

"Never mind kid. Run along, I'll see you soon."

Every day after that, Kevin snuck some food from work and fed the homeless man. One afternoon Kevin decided to stop and spend some time talking with the man. As he walked the familiar route, he saw the man in his usual spot. Kevin had brought along some warm apple pie and a homemade chicken pot pie. As he approached, he yelled out, "Hey, I brought you some chicken pot pie and some more apple pie!"

"Oh, so I get two pies today? How nice of you!"

"Do you mind if I sit down?" Kevin asked.

"No, go right ahead, have a seat in my living room." Both men laughed. "Sorry I never thanked you for saving me the other day, or for the food. I get kind of suspicious of people sometimes. I didn't mean any harm. By the way, my name is Passion."

"Hello Passion, are you homeless?"

"Yes, the person I was living with kicked me out, leaving me with no place to go; but I'd rather not talk about that right now."

"I understand why you don't trust people. Neither do I."

"Hmmm, yes, I see. But I think we have very different reasons."

"How so?" Kevin asked.

"You have trust issues and keep people at bay. I trust everyone and give them a chance. Even after they abandon me, I find a way to forgive them."

"So why do you continue to trust people if they disappoint you?"

"When you love people, you try to help them, even if they do disappoint you at times. Never allow what someone did to you in the past, to prevent you from helping other people in the present. Sometimes our past experiences can shape how we see the world, and how we see people. You can never be your best self if you live in constant fear of people. Love and hate cannot occupy the same heart," Passion continued.

Speaking with Passion gave Kevin hope. Each day when he got off work, he would take the long route home so he could have a conversation with Passion. Although Kevin hadn't known Passion long, he mustered up the courage to ask Passion to come live with him. After all, Kevin had plenty of space in his one-bedroom apartment. It would be nice having someone to talk to on nights when he couldn't sleep or when he had a bad day at work. When Kevin asked Passion if he would like to be his roommate; Passion agreed.

Kevin hadn't lived with anyone since moving from his mother's house. Living with someone felt strange again. Kevin was initially cautious around Passion, due to his painful childhood. He remembered Passion's advice and decided not to allow his past to over shadow his life.

In the meantime, Passion settled into his new place. He finally had somewhere to live, and knew he had to be on his best behavior. He did not want to do anything that would cause Kevin to get rid of him. The two men grew close. Kevin looked forward to the stories Passion told. Passion gave Kevin energy. He made Kevin reflect on his life and his journey.

The more time Kevin spent with Passion, the more he disliked his current life. He dreaded going to work, and often wondered how he ended up at such a dead-end job after all he had been through. Kevin began to question his future and wondered if he would ever be happy. Just then, Passion rounded the corner carrying a bag of freshly popped popcorn.

He asked, "So Kevin, what do you want to get into tonight?"

He noticed the somber look on Kevin's face. "Oh no, not you, too! I will get my bags and leave."

"No wait! Where are you going?"

Passion told Kevin, "I have seen that look before. It's the look people give me right before they get rid of me."

Kevin begged Passion not to leave. Later on that night, Kevin understood why so many people did not want to live with Passion. He had a way of making people want more out of life and often caused them to take inventory of the life they were living.

Finally, it was the last work day of the week. Kevin felt relieved; he would have the next couple of days off to relax. He wanted to do something with Passion, so they could feel closer. He had little money and knew of no place interesting he could take Passion. So, he invited Passion to come to work with him. It would be nice to introduce Passion to all his co-workers and maybe to a few of the customers. But first he had to clean Passion up. He looked a hot mess! Kevin went into his closet and found a sweat suit that would fit. He returned to the living room and told Passion to get dressed.

"What for?" Passion asked.

"You are coming to work with me. I want you to meet my friends."

Passion chuckled, "Nice sweat suit, but I am not going to work with you."

"Why not?" Kevin asked. "It is not like you have a lot to do. Don't you get bored just sitting around doing nothing?"

"Actually, I stay quite busy avoiding negative people and preserving my energy. I don't just go around meeting people, Kevin. I must be sought after and embraced. Do you know how hard it would be trying to force myself upon people? In fact, I must depart from you soon, Kevin, unless you find something for me to do."

"I am trying to get you to come to my job. Why won't you come?"

"Because I will cause you to lose your job."

"How would you do that? I think you might actually liven up the place a bit. I could especially use your help with my grouchy manager."

"Kevin, I have met your manager before and he doesn't care for me. Remember I told you he ran me away and threatened to call the police on me if I didn't leave. You see I met him when he was fresh out of college looking for a job. When he couldn't find the job of his choice, he abandoned me. He told me he never wanted to be friends with me again. He accused me of being a liar. He said I made people want things that were not possible. I tried to reason with him, but he threatened to tell everyone I was a fraud. So, I left him alone and vowed never to be friends with anyone else unless they really wanted me."

"So why would you even come home with me if you knew you were not going to stay?" Kevin asked.

Passion grabbed Kevin's arm and led him to the sofa. "Have a seat Kevin, we need to talk. You need to understand that by just having me around will not make your life better. When you get close to me and began to listen to what I have to say, you will lose friends and sometimes family."

"Really? I don't understand why people would not like you."

"You see Kevin, people actually love me. That is until they see what it cost to really have me in their lives. Only a few people are really committed to having a friendship with me. I meet a lot of interesting people. Some of them are famous and have done very well for themselves. I am still friends with a lot of people who have befriended me."

"Like who?" Kevin asked, leaning forward on the couch.

"Oprah Winfrey, Steve Harvey, Ellen DeGeneres, and former President Barack Obama, just to name a few."

Kevin stood up in disbelief. "No way! Can you please introduce me to some of the people you know?"

"If you decide you want to stay friends with me, you will encounter many successful people. But my friendship comes with a cost. When I come around, things change and not always for the better. What was once acceptable now becomes unacceptable. I remind people that there is much more to life than just surviving. Remember how we met; that is why the group of boys were fighting me. When they saw me in their neighborhood, they said I didn't belong. I was surprised that you came to my rescue. Most people just ignore me, and act as if I don't even exist. These words reminded Kevin of his forgotten dream to once become invisible.

Kevin told Passion, "You remind me of a friend I met some time ago. Her name is Love."

Passion began laughing.

"What's funny? Do you know Love?"
"I should. She gave birth to me."

Kevin eyes widened. "Wait a minute, did you say Love gave birth to you?"

"Yes, Love is my mother." ·

Confused, Kevin asked, "If Love birthed you, why doesn't she care for you?"

"Just like a baby in the womb, once I began to grow, I could not be contained. And as I grew up, Love had to let me grow on my own. I am sure she taught you about the importance of separation. Nothing we birth truly belongs to us but is meant to make the world a better place. You are a gift to the world, and you must not hide from it. None of us belong to ourselves or a small group of select people. In fact, I am your friend, but I do not belong so much to you as I belong to your gift.

Scratching his head, Kevin asked, "So, I need you, Passion, for my gift?"

"Yes, that is the only way your gift will survive in the world and do what it was created to do."

"If you had not found me, your gift would be useless."

"Hmm, I didn't know I needed passion for my gift. So, I found you because I needed you?"

"I wouldn't exactly say you found me, you simply noticed me."

"But I did. I stumbled upon you getting trampled and I came to your rescue."

Passion smiled. "No Kevin, I came to your rescue! Do you remember what you were thinking about when you noticed me?"

"I think so. I was walking and thinking about how unhappy I was with my job.

"Bingo! Your discontentment made you turn and look in my direction. If you think about it, you noticed the three kids first. Those kids are from a gang called Misery. They run in groups and look for people to beat up. You see, it was I who saved you. Your unhappiness attracted Misery to you. They were on their way to attack you when I intervened. If I had not stepped in to protect you, they would have ganged up on you. Your life would have never been the same if they had gotten a hold of you. I ran toward you. They were attempting to stop me from getting to you. The only thing that scared them off is you coming toward me."

"So, when I ran toward you, I chased away the Misery gang? Kevin asked.

"Yes Kevin!"

Knowing Passion was telling the truth, Kevin's legs grew weak, and he lowered himself into the recliner nearby. He was now facing Passion. He hated to admit it, but Passion was right. Kevin put his head in his hands. He could feel tears forming, but he didn't want Passion to see him cry. Passion got up from the couch and approached Kevin. He placed his hand on Kevin's shoulder. He immediately snatched his hand away. Passion could feel the negative energy coming from Kevin's body. It almost knocked him unconscious. "Whoa!" Passion screamed as he staggered backwards.

Kevin jumped up. "What? What's wrong?"

"Son, if you want me to hang around, you must change that attitude of yours because your negative attitude is draining me."

"I'm sorry. It's just that everything is so hard."

"Yes, life is hard, but your attitude makes it more difficult. You must look at your challenges with a different attitude."

Passion then suggested, "Why don't you take some time off work and follow me around for a week. I want to show you what it's like to follow me."

"Follow you? But I found you, so how are you going to show me around?

"This is true. You did find me, but ever since I've been with you, you have done nothing but ask me to follow you around. You always want to make suggestions, but you haven't listened to me once! That's your problem, you are a horrible listener! You love to gather information, thinking it will make you successful, but real success comes from being able to hear. You must be able to listen to your life."

Passion could sense that his last statement confused Kevin. "I will make you a deal. If you come somewhere with me, then I promise I will go to work with you. But I have a feeling after following me, you will not want to return to your job."

Kevin agreed.

Passion led Kevin to a large mountain. Once they got to the base of the mountain, Passion told Kevin there was someone he wanted him to meet. Kevin began to look around anxiously and asked, "What time will he or she arrive?"

"They're not coming to us, we must go and meet them."

"Where is this person located?" asked Kevin.

Passion looked up and pointed to the top of the mountain.

"WHAT!" screamed Kevin. "There is no way I am going up there!"

"Welcome to Mt. Challenge. This is where you will meet the final person on your journey."

"So, you were born at a place called Mt. Challenge?" Kevin asked.

"Enough with the questions already, just follow me!"

As they trudged halfway along their journey, Passion told Kevin it was time to take a break. They found a cave to rest in, but neither of them could sleep. Kevin was curious about why Passion had left home.

Sensing Kevin wanted to take a trip down "Memory Lane," Passion jumped to his feet suggesting that Kevin follow him through the cave to see what they could find. As they began to explore, they noticed some paintings on the wall. They were the most beautiful paintings Kevin had ever seen. As they continued further, they discovered more and more beautiful paintings on the walls and on the ceilings of the cave. Kevin marveled at the detail of the artwork. He wondered to himself, *who would hide such beautiful art in such a dark and hidden place?*

Distracted by the paintings, Kevin was startled by Passion tugging on his shoulder. Passion pointed Kevin in the direction of a female figure with her back to them. She had a paintbrush in hand and was painting on the wall. Stunned, Kevin asked, "How can she make ordinary things look so beautiful?"

"I don't know so let's ask her." Before they could move toward the figure, she spoke, "Hello there!"

Kevin wondered, *how did she know we were here?*

The woman laughed, "Because you were talking behind my back! Hello, my name is Creativity."

Kevin asked, "Did you create all of this?"
"Sure, I did. I can create anything. That's how I got my name."

"But how did you do so much with so little?"

"Where you see little, I see plenty. You viewed this as a dark cave with ugly rocks. I saw it as a blank canvas for my imagination. I turned what you saw as useless, into something that others could admire. Have you ever done that Kevin?"

Wow! How did you know my name?"

"Your friend said it while you both were speaking."

"So, you heard us?"

"No Kevin, I heard Passion."

"So, you couldn't hear me?"

"No, I can only hear Passion."

"But you are talking to me now," Kevin argued.

Creativity laughed, "No, Passion is speaking for you."

"So, you can only hear me if Passion interprets what I say?"

"Bingo! You see, without Passion, you would have never met me. Passion led you to me. Look around Kevin. Have you taken notice of where you found me?"

Kevin looked around, "A dark cave?"

Grabbing Kevin's hand, Creativity responded, "Yes, I am always found in dark places. You must be willing to travel in the darkness to connect with me. Many people don't meet me because they are afraid of the dark. They depend too much on their eyes and what they see. Only when you are bold enough to go toward what you cannot see will you find me." Creativity turned around and began walking. Kevin followed with Passion walking between the two of them.

As they made their way up the mountain, Kevin followed Passion and Creativity as if his life depended on it. Every now and then, he looked down at how far they had climbed. Kevin wanted to return to the bottom of the mountain, but noticed he was too far up to turn around.

They came upon a ledge that was difficult to cross. Passion stopped alongside Creativity as Kevin brought up the rear.

"What now?" Kevin shouted. Passion told Creativity, "I guess this is a good place to stop, set up camp and get some rest." Kevin unrolled his sleeping bag and laid in the dark until he dozed off.

The next morning Kevin awoke to Passion and Creativity staring at him. He sat up, stretched, and began to get out of his sleeping bag. "What?" Kevin asked.

"We are waiting for you to tell us what to do."

"Huh? Tell you what to do? Passion got us into this mess. We are on Mt. Challenge because of Passion, and now you're asking for my guidance?"

"Yes, we can only take you so far, and then the rest of the journey is up to you. The only way we can conquer this great mountain and introduce you to the final step of your journey is if you lead us."

Kevin reluctantly led the way up until they finally reached the top. He looked around and saw Creativity and Passion smiling at him.

"What is so funny?" Kevin asked.

"We are not laughing at you. We are happy to see an old friend of ours!"

Kevin turned around and saw a tall beautiful figure. He noticed the figure had no face, just a silhouette of a person. The figure spoke first, "Hello Kevin, glad to see you finally made it. I didn't think you'd get here"

"Purpose?"
"Yes. I am the reason you were born."

"But why don't you have a face?" Kevin asked.

"Because I look different to each person who encounters me. My image will become clearer to you over time. But you must follow me no matter where I lead you. The moment you turn back or doubt my instructions, I will begin to fade away. Come closer as I want to show you the view of the world from up here."

While hanging out with Purpose on the top of Mt. Challenge, Kevin felt like he was on top of the world.

"Wow! Has the world always been this beautiful?"

"Yes," Purpose replied.
"Why haven't I noticed it?"

Purpose responded, "All things look different when you find me."

"So why are you so difficult to reach?" asked Kevin.

"I am not difficult to find, but most people do not want to go through what you did to find me. Most people want me to come find them and introduce myself."

"So, I would never have found you if I had not climbed Mt. Challenge?"

"You would have never found me if you did not embark on your journey in the Healing Forest, through the revealing wilderness, or your climb of Mt. Challenge. They all worked together to help you discover me, Purpose. Which part of your journey proved to be the most difficult for you?"

Kevin replied, "It was climbing this big mountain. I saw how big and scary it looked. I was intimidated by it. Little did I know climbing it would lead me to you."

Purpose laughed at Kevin. "Have you ever heard of the story of David and Goliath?"

"Yes," replied Kevin. "Isn't that about a small shepherd boy who fights a giant warrior?"

"Most people see that story as a David fighting a giant, but they miss the message in the story."

"And what is the message?" asked Kevin.

"It's simple. In order to find your purpose, you must be willing to fight something bigger than yourself. David would never have seen his potential to be king, or found his purpose in leading a nation, if he was not willing to fight something bigger than himself. So yes, this mountain was bigger than you, and you had to conquer it to find me. However, I sense there is something bigger you were born to fight.

Kevin paused and thought for a moment. He looked at Purpose and wondered aloud, "But what?"

Purpose continued, "When you were a child something happened to you. Do you know what I am referring to?"

"Yes, I was kidnapped and made to do awful things."

"How did you escape?"
"I fought off the guy who assaulted me."
"Yes, what you had to fight to survive, is a clue as to why you were born. You fought off an abuser. Now your job is to help other victims fight and survive their abuse. You were born to fight abuse."

Kevin's eyes widened. It was like someone had grabbed a hold of his spirit. "So, is that why I don't like to see people unhappy, or why I get angry when people are abused?

"Yes, that is part of it. You see, a lot of people in the world have been abused and are not aware of it. Abuse stops us from being ourselves. Happiness is about being free to be ourselves, and nothing separates us from being ourselves more than abuse. Somehow you knew this, and it made you sad. When you saw other people living unhappy lives, it touched the unhappy little boy inside of you. The little boy tried to get you to pay attention to other people's unhappiness because you were ignoring his."

Kevin looked to the ground in deep thought, "So the abused little boy inside of me wanted me to reconnect with him so I could be happy?"

"Yes. Until that happens, you cannot help others heal their inner child. This is what it means to be born again. It means to nurture our inner child. This is where all our wisdom, creativity, and courage come from."

"If that is true, why do adults' control everything and children have no power?"

Purpose drew closer to Kevin and looked him square in the eye. "That is what your whole journey has been about. It was to get you to understand an important truth: we are never closer to God than when we are children. The world teaches us that when our bodies grow, we must ignore our inner child. Many people like you have been hurt as children. They can't wait to become an adult. They think that by being an adult they will forget all their childhood pain. However, this is not true. You see, once a child is abused, their spirit remains trapped at the age of the abuse. The person's body grows, but their spirit is put in a prison of sorts. In order to live a fulfilling life, the person must go back and free the child from prison. All the great teachers knew this great fact. Even Jesus said, "Unless you change and become like little children, you will never fulfill your potential."

Suddenly, Kevin found himself standing in an open field. He heard a small squeaky voice coming from below. He looked in the direction of the voice and saw a small person the size of a flower looking up at him. Kevin squinted, he could barely see the person. The more he stared at the figure, the larger it grew. The figure grew until it was hovering over Kevin, who had to shield his eyes from the sun to look up at the figure. It was a man. His features looked familiar, but Kevin couldn't quite place him. Although he was a stranger, Kevin felt like he knew him.

Hey Kevin, did you meet Potential?"
"Potential? No, I never met him."

"Are you sure? He has been with you all your life. In fact, he was the one who started you on this journey of discovery."

"The man under the bridge and on the plane?"
"Bingo!"

"Why did he look like a bomb under the bridge and only a little better on the plane?"

"Your potential looks exactly how you picture it. On that fateful day when you decided to look at your Potential rather than ignore him, he spoke to you. Potential was only invisible because you made him that way. When you acknowledged him, he spoke to you! You see, you had to come to this field to hear him again. This field is called the Land of Possibilities. In this space, you can hear a pin drop because everything is in the open. There are no boundaries."

Kevin whispered, "So is that why I was able to hear Potential's small voice?"

"Exactly! And the more you stared at Potential while listening to him…."

Kevin interrupted, "The larger he grew! So, that is what Passion meant about being able to hear. Once I took my mind off my limitations, only then would I be able to hear Potential. My world was over crowded with worry and concern, preventing me from hearing Potential, who was with me the whole time. By standing next to Purpose, I was able to focus. As a result, I could hear Potential speak to me. That would mean this Land of Possibilities, or this open field, represents an open mind."

"By God, I think the boy has got it!" Purpose shouted. "Now that you see things from a different perspective, are you ready to return to your life? You can't stay on this mountain top forever."

"Yes, but not without you, my Purpose."

"I cannot follow you Kevin. You can only carry me with you in your heart. I do not force myself onto people, instead, they must be willing to take my hand. Very few have come this high up the mountain and have come to know me. Even fewer have taken my hand and carried me back to the real word in their hearts. Many times, my journey down the mountain is often cut short when people forget me or ignore me to seek a simple existence. That on its own is an unholy act," Purpose told him.

"Unholy act? That was what Passion said to me," Kevin replied emphatically. For so long, Kevin had searched for Purpose, without even knowing it. He had searched for something else in the healing forest and in the wilderness. He felt his heart bloom with gratitude to those who had helped him along his way.

"I see a familiar smile on your face. It is the look of ease, a desire to rest now that you have come to know me; but your journey is only just beginning. When we get to the bottom of the mountain, you will not see me by your side anymore for I will be ahead of you waiting for you to find me."

"But you are here now; I know you. Why do I still have to find you? Why do you have to leave me?"

"Because the closer we get back to your reality, the less tangible I will become to you. Your mind will be riddled with the simple problems of the real world; trivial beings who seek to become bigger and worshipped. You will have to strive to make me real as well. I am but an illusion now. I can only be of use to you if I am tangible. Find me and I will help lead you on your path to Happiness."

"But I am happy now," Kevin said. As though a dark cloud covered them, Purpose's demeanor changed for a moment and he loomed over Kevin. His voice was raspy and almost inaudible. "There is a greater happiness Kevin. Never allow yourself to get too comfortable in a position until you find me. Even though you have known me and know how to find me, you will still meet obstacles and people who wish to keep you down. You might meet Failure on the way, but do not be dejected by his presence. It only means you are getting closer to finding me," Purpose told him.

Kevin couldn't quite remember the frown that had clouded Purpose's face minutes before. It was gone without a trace. All that lingered was the aura around Purpose, the sense of fulfillment. However, according to Purpose, this was simply the beginning of another journey.

"Now we must go," Passion spoke for the first time in a while. Kevin had forgotten the presence of both Passion and Creativity.

"He is going to leave me at the foot of the mountain. What about the two of you?" Kevin asked them.

"I shall return with you until you do not need me anymore," Passion said to him.

"I will never send you away to live on the streets again. Besides, you have grown on me," Kevin argued, but Passion said nothing.

"I cannot stay idle or dormant, nor can I belong to only one person. Though I will always be there when you need me," Creativity said with a reassuring smile. Kevin, who had been happy only moments before learning of his new friend's departures, now felt a little downcast.

"Chin up Kevin. The climb down the mountain is a little more crowded than the climb up. You will need a smile to ward off the trespassers," Purpose told him as he came to his side. "Some of them you have met before. Come now and let us commence on our journey to finding one another."

Purpose put out his hand to Kevin, whose hand was completely covered by Purpose's large grip. Kevin glanced to his side and saw that Purpose was also much taller than when they first met.

Why is he taller now? Kevin wondered.

"I am taller to you because you are dreaming. I only appear as you see me. It is good to dream, but do not let me grow so much that you are unable to keep up with my stride. If I grow, then you too must grow."

With that, the two started their climb down from the mountain's peak. Kevin held onto Purpose's large hand which seemed to emit a radiating warmth that enveloped Kevin's entire body keeping him warm as the sun slowly fell from the sky, and the chill of the night air settled in. Passion and Creativity walked closely behind the two as they all descended slowly.

"Can we stop now?" Kevin asked his traveling companions. "My legs are weak, and my eyes are weary."

"We shall rest then. Passion, you will build a fire to keep us warm," directed Purpose as he brought Kevin to a clearing with a large tent. The four climbers entered the tent and found beds and food.

"Who do we have to thank for this?" Kevin asked, but none of his companions answered. They seemed a bit leery of the luxury and comfort of the tent. It was almost like the forbidding feeling that had come upon Anger, Fear, Shame, and Guilt when Hope had first shown herself to Kevin. *Trouble*, they had called her.

"Is the food poisonous?" Kevin asked Purpose. They shook their heads no. Kevin shrugged and helped himself to some roasted chicken.

"I would advise you not to eat that," Purpose said.

"Why? You said the food was not poisonous, and I am famished!" His stomach rumbled so loud that he feared they all could hear it.

"You don't know who provided this tent or the food. Nothing in life is free. Everything comes with a price."

"What price must we pay for this strange comfort in the mountains?" Kevin inquired.

Passion was the only one who dared to come close to him. Kevin hadn't noticed that Purpose wasn't holding his hand anymore. He had been too distracted by his own needs and the comfort of the tent that he had forgotten his companions.

"This is a gift to all of us; I can feel it," Kevin said as he climbed into one of the five beds in the tent. "Relax, there is nothing to fear."

Creativity, Passion, and Purpose reluctantly sat on the other beds leaving one for the stranger who owned the tent and the food. Purpose lay on the bed nearest the entrance of the tent, and farthest from Kevin.

Soon there was no noise to be heard within the tent. Outside, there was only the nocturnal sound of the crickets crying out their songs of worship to the moon goddess.

***

Kevin awoke to the sound of thunder. It was drizzling outside the tent. He could tell by the dark hue that was cast inside the tent. His companions were asleep, unperturbed by the cold or the thunder. Kevin tried to go back to sleep, but he couldn't get comfortable. So, he got up and made his way to the entrance of the tent. The rain was but a meek drizzle as he had expected, though the sound of thunder was odd, given the weakness of the sky's outpour.

Against his better judgment, Kevin ventured out into the rain. It seemed unbelievable at first, but he thought he could hear his name in the rumble of the thunder that ravaged the peace of the night. *Kevin*, it thundered again. The lightning that marked the sky always dissolved somewhere ahead in the woods. Curious, Kevin found himself walking towards the area of the woods where the lighting had struck the earth. *What drew the lightning to the earth?* Kevin wondered as he moved towards what could only be danger.

Do not go out at night after 7:00 p.m., you should be in your room. Do not go near the woods alone, an animal could maul you. Stay away from shops late at night, they might get robbed and you could get caught in the crossfire....

These were the words of warning spoken by Kevin's mother and his family, often played over and over in his head. Kevin's mom lived her entire life running away from danger. In many ways, she was afraid of too many things, that she never actually enjoyed the pleasures therein.

Kevin was slowly developing those same characteristics. He used to be fearful of storms, but something about the lightning intrigued him. Almost as if it called out to him, saying his name, so he walked towards it.

Coming out of a cluster of trees, Kevin came to a lake where a man was seated near the water. He could not see the man's face for his back was turned towards him.

Next to the man was a wicker basket from which a cobra danced in the starlight. *A snake charmer*, thought Kevin. The man was dressed in a robe, with a turban wrapped around his head. The man brought his flute to his lips each time a lightning bolt struck the lake. The heave of the man's shoulders told Kevin when the man blew into his flute, but the loud claps of thunder seemed to drown out the sound of the flute. The cobra frequently hissed in anger as it danced rhythmically to the music, but it never attacked the charmer.

"Why do you stay out in the night? Come, there is a tent with an empty bed not far away," Kevin called to the snake charmer.

"I have to be out here lest we not have the opportunity to talk alone, Kevin," the snake charmer said as he rose to his feet. He wasn't a tall man. He was stocky and his large turban was wrapped heavily around his neck and head, almost concealing his face. Even though it was dark, and Kevin could barely see the man's face, there was something slightly familiar about the man's voice that Kevin could not quite place.

"How do you know my name and why do you wish to speak to me alone?" Kevin became wary, sticking to the protection of the trees instead of venturing out towards the snake charmer and the lake.

"We have met before though you were slightly younger then. It wasn't so long ago that you should be able to remember," the snake charmer said.

Suddenly, another bolt of lightning struck the lake and the charmer hurriedly put the flute to his lips and blew. Again, the thunder struck, and Kevin heard no sound from the flute.

"It must be exhausting playing the flute but not hearing it," Kevin remarked. The man laughed before drawing closer to Kevin, who kept his distance from the snake charmer.

"You worry because you dream. You imagine that the sound of the flute must be something you know, something you are familiar with, but you fail to see what is right in front of you. I make the thunder," the snake charmer said.

Another bolt of lightning struck the lake, but this time the snake charmer did not put his flute to his mouth, and there was no thunder. As though to prove his point to Kevin, he put the flute to his mouth and blew. The skies roared with thunder. In that moment, Kevin realized the snake charmer was indeed telling the truth; that he was the one responsible for causing the thundering sound.

"Wow! How do you do that?" Kevin asked him.

"I do not know. It is just the way you humans perceive the sound of my flute. Come out of the trees and let us talk, Kevin. I have much to tell you," the snake charmer waved at him, but Kevin could not go near him. There was a negative aura around the man that scared Kevin or perhaps it was the cobra in the basket that scared at him.

"Come now, I will not harm you. We are friends, remember? It is I, Fear," the man said to Kevin holding out his hand.

Ah yes, Kevin remembered now where he had heard the voice before. It was in the Healing Forest. It had been a long while since he had seen Fear, Shame, and the lot of Fear's friends. Summoning up his strength, Kevin ventured out of the protection of the trees and drew closer to Fear.

"You abandoned us, your friends. We all wanted to come with you. I eventually was elected to come find you, as I was the most likely one that you would talk to." Fear walked back to the lake and Kevin followed, feeling more at ease.

"I have journeyed with you for a long time waiting for you to come to me, but you never did."

"I'm sorry I left all of you but Hope and her sisters made me feel better. You and your friends made me feel, well, invisible. I like my new friends. They set me on a path to find Purpose, and now I have to thank them," Kevin apologized. Fear merely nodded his head in acceptance. "Then why didn't you ever call to me all the while you followed me?"

"I cannot seek you, only you can seek me out," Fear answered. He sat on his mat by the cobra as Kevin sat next to him.

"Are you the owner of the tent?"

"Yes, I provided the shelter and the food for you. I knew the journey was long and more treacherous at night. In the morning you can continue your way. Perhaps, I might tag along if you wish."

Kevin said nothing because he wasn't so sure someone like Fear would be readily accepted into their journey party.

"While you think about that, I did say I had a lot to talk to you about," Fear continued. "I always knew there was something special about you. I have watched you follow the path that Hope outlined for you. Along the way you met Failure. He doesn't like me very much because people prefer my company to his. I only began to get worried when you met Passion."

"Why," Kevin asked.

"Passion makes people dream and forget what is right in front of them. If you follow him long enough, I know he will eventually bring you to see Creativity and Purpose. Beware of Purpose, as he will make you feel good for a moment, give you a sense of fulfillment, but it's dangerous. He is a con man, playing games with the lives of humans. Many are lucky not to find him. The few that do, he toys with them. He makes them lust after him and then he disappears urging them to find him. Many have searched years for him; while some die never seeing his face again. I'm sure he finds pleasure when they don't succeed in relocating him."

"I was told by Passion himself, that when I find him, he will lead me to Happiness," said Kevin reassuringly.

"He'll help you find Happiness; is that what he told you? My dear boy, Happiness is everywhere! You only have to be content with what you have, what is real and right in front of you." Fear lowered himself to his knees and stared into the lake. He motioned for Kevin to do the same. The rain and lightning had stopped.

"Look into the lake and you will see your path to Happiness. He is closer than you think," Fear told him.

Kevin crouched on all fours and peered into the lake. He saw himself becoming the manager at his place of work. The image of him in the lake was happy. Soon, he had a wife and three beautiful children. Over time, they all grew old together.

"Who is that? I can see a shadow moving about me in the water," Kevin pointed into the lake.

"That is Happiness," Fear replied. Kevin smiled and returned his focus to the water. The longer he looked, the less he could see the shadow, but its presence was still there.

Suddenly, Fear slapped the surface of the water causing multiple ripples, and the images quickly disappeared.

"It almost seemed like Happiness was fading away the older I became," Kevin observed.

"It is that way with Happiness. He never stays too long, but he is a blessing for as long as he does. Many are lucky to even have him so close, to see his face before they leave this world. Believe me when I say that having him for that length of time is long enough. You might want to discuss all of this with Purpose.

However, knowing Purpose, she would say otherwise. You are not the first to seek me out after meeting Purpose. Not many can endure her games, riddles, and promises. Happiness will only stick around when you find Purpose. He is attracted to her, and he feels lonely when she is not around. Can't you see Kevin, Happiness is following you, hoping you can lead him to the love of his life, Purpose. Instead of trying to find Happiness, place all your focus on Purpose, and Happiness will surely come around. Do you know how long it will take you to find Purpose?"

Kevin thought for a moment and became sullen realizing he didn't know the answer to this question. Fear began to grip him. *What if he never found Purpose once they got to the foot of the mountain?*

"Sure, she would promise that Happiness would stay with you forever, but as the saying goes, a bird in hand is worth more than two in the bush. You must choose a path, one of certainty or that of Purpose. Both might take a long time, but my way is definite. The manager at your place of employment is threatened by you, and the more he shows his insecurities, the more people will likely turn to you to take his place. That's when you will find Happiness and he will be with you for a while. Should you choose to follow Purpose, I cannot tell you how long that will take or if you'd ever find her."

As much as Kevin wanted to believe Fear, he could not change the way Purpose made him feel. There was a genuine warmth that enveloped Kevin when he was around Purpose instead of feeling the cold and rain that accompanied Fear. However, Fear did have a point. How long would it take to find Purpose? Kevin was certain that Purpose had not lied to him when she said she would lead him to Happiness.

"I'm cold," Kevin muttered under his breath. "Is there more that you wanted to tell me?"

Fear rose to his feet, and Kevin did the same.

"What's the significance of the cobra?" Kevin asked of Fear, the snake charmer.

"The significance is the venom. It is the only thing that can kill beings like us. I brought it in case you had the need for it."

"Why would I need to kill any of you?" Kevin was startled by Fear's insinuations. The cobra was now in a defensive position and was intently staring at Fear. Kevin, now aware of the snake's stance, had no idea if it were waiting for a command to strike and kill.

"Now that you know the truth, your friends might not be so happy to have you as their travelling companion. They may seek to trap you, leaving the cobra as your only of escape back to life as you know it on your quest to find Happiness. I know you are not a killer; therefore, I would take responsibility if you so wish. It would be said that 'Fear killed Passion, Creativity, and Purpose, not Kevin.' Think over your options and meet me here in the morning with your decision," Fear said to Kevin dryly.

Troubled by the sinister turn of their conversation, Kevin bid Fear a goodnight, and hurried back to the tent. He hadn't walked far away from the lake before the rain started again; now much stronger than before. He entered the tent to find his companions still fast asleep. They had not noticed his absence. Kevin quietly climbed back into his bed and pulled the blankets over his head. Trying to escape what had transpired by the lake, he prayed that sleep would overtake him quickly, but it wasn't forthcoming. The sound of thunder outside was a continued reminder of the decision that Kevin had to make by morning.

***

"Wake up Kevin, its morning; wake up, it's time to go."

Kevin felt hands nudge him gently out of his slumber. He couldn't recall falling asleep the night before.

"We have a long way to go," Passion reminded him. "You seem distant, what is it?" Purpose stepped forward to look at Kevin squarely. Kevin told them about his encounter with Fear. He had expected a look of horror or despair on their faces at the mention of the cobra, but they seemed passive.

"Fear might come to kill you all if I don't meet him this morning as promised." Kevin voiced his dilemma and was still surprised by their calm demeanor.

Purpose spoke up, "We knew it was only a matter of time before Fear showed up. He always waits for the select few who eventually meet me. Fear can only kill us if you let him. He is not as powerful as he appears. He needs you to succumb to his false teachings in order to mislead you. If you do, it will be you that kills us, not him. Fear is powerless—unless you allow him to use you Kevin."

"But he showed me my future; I saw Happiness." Kevin had dreamt about the vision Fear had shown him all night.

"It is a ploy by Fear."

"But it felt real," Kevin interrupted. Passion had a look of terror come over his face as he watched Kevin dabble in worry and indecision.

"It is one of your possible futures. We are all born with one true path to follow; but since we are granted the gift of free will, we are allowed to decide which path we shall choose. Every single decision we make is a step forward or backward along our paths. What Fear showed you was a possible future that could easily be yours, but that depends on the decisions you make today."

Kevin couldn't find any more clarity in his decision.

Purpose continued, "The question is one of self-belief. How long a man's path, reflects the value of his self-belief. Finding me did not depend on you. Many invite Fear along because they think their search for me will be long and tedious with many obstacles they don't know how to overcome. Do you believe in yourself?"

"How can I believe in myself?" questioned Kevin with a tear in his eye.

"I am you, Kevin. I am what you are destined to become. If you believe in me, then you will find me and become one with me. Once you accomplish this, I will lead you to Happiness, and he will stay with you forever. Were you able to see Happiness's face in Fear's vision?"

Kevin shook his head no. "I could feel his presence, but the older I grew, the less I felt it. It seemed as if he was fading away to nothingness. I asked Fear about this, but he told me not everyone can have Happiness forever. He said I would be lucky to have him for as long as I could in the vision."

"I will ask again. Did you see Happiness's face in the vision?" Purpose asked with a bright smile that reminded Kevin of

Gratitude. Purpose spoke again before Kevin could shake his head, affirming what Purpose already knew.

"If he had shown you Happiness's face, then you would not have become so conflicted. That is how Fear operates; he only shows you what he needs to in order to control you. Let's go down the mountain Kevin, and then you shall see the face of Happiness. You shall have his company forever. But you will have to choose."

Kevin puffed out his chest in sheer determination, he had decided. "I have made my choice. I am going with you," Kevin told his three companions. Passion and Creativity were elated, but the look on Purpose's face was still passive.

Purpose spoke again, "Remember the words of Hope, Kevin. You cannot run away from Fear, as he will always come after you. You must overcome Fear, leave Shame, get rid of Guilt, and ultimately face Pain. If you don't accomplish this, Fear will surface later when you have left the mountain. Down there, he might be harder to overcome if you do not have a strong resolve."

Kevin nodded and walked past them to tell Fear he had made his decision. Just a few feet away from the tent stood Fear with the basket and the cobra.

"What decision have you come to, Kevin? One of reality or that of a pipe dream?" Fear said coldly. Though Kevin had been confident enough to speak about his decision while inside the tent, he now had a hard time saying it in the presence of Fear.

I choose Purpose, Kevin thought.

"You have to say it!" Fear shouted to him.

"I choose Purpose," Kevin muttered under his breath.

"I cannot hear you, louder!" demanded Fear.

"I choose Purpose," Kevin said, but even he doubted his own voice.

"I do not sense resolution in your tone Kevin. Perhaps you need more time to come to a decision. I will always be here. My tent, the bed, and the food, will all be here for you for as long as you need, until you can tell me what you really want."

Kevin began to consider this option. Perhaps he needed more time to think and be sure of his decision. But even he knew what he was choosing, which was running from Fear and hiding. He looked back at Purpose, Passion, and Creativity. Of the three of them, Passion was still the most expressive. It seemed that only he truly feared for Kevin.

Passion felt compelled to speak, "I cannot stay in the middle of this for too long Kevin. Unlike you who are mortal, I do not have much time on my side. I can only be at the top of the mountain where you can seek me momentarily, or at the bottom where you can seek me still and become one with me."

Kevin turned back to Fear, but he couldn't look him in the eye. The cobra raised its head eagerly.

Fear spoke up, "They only wish to confuse you. They only seek to hold you back, trap you in a fantasy that even they cannot confirm would become a reality. They are liars and thus deserve to die! Give the word and I will punish them, thereby freeing you from this mountain, so you can go and find Happiness." Fear had his flute ready.

"What does Happiness look like?" Kevin asked Fear.

"What did you say?" Fear shouted louder than Kevin had. He had hoped to intimidate Kevin with his tone, forcing him to be quiet about his question, but Kevin raised his voice even louder.

"What does Happiness look like?"

"You saw him in the lake just as I did. You felt his presence just as I did."

"I think the reason I could not see his face in the lake was because you have never actually met Happiness. You have never seen his face before, have you?" inquired Kevin. Fear said nothing but took a step back towards the trees from whence he had come.

"You didn't answer me, Fear. Perhaps you did not hear me. You have never seen Happiness before, have you?" Fear took another step backwards. Kevin was exhilarated as he could feel the smile that spread across his own face. *You will need a smile to ward off trespassers*, Purpose had told him.

"I choose Purpose," Kevin told Fear boldly. "I choose the unknown for it is known to me. It is me, it is my destiny."

Fear paused and then said, "I will leave you be this day. My offer still stands, even when you return home. I will come to you whenever you call me. I hope you will have had a change of heart when next we cross paths. People always have a change of heart. Until we meet again...." Fear picked up his cobra and went back into the woods.

Kevin walked back to join his companions, but the tent was gone along with the furniture and the food.

Purpose explained, "What you feel now is a bit of Happiness. You have conquered Fear yet again. We should continue on our journey before the sun is no longer on our side."

"Why is the tent gone?" Kevin asked as they made their way steadily down the mountain hand-in-hand.

"That is the way of Fear. He scares people from moving forward and continuing along their journey. He makes them afraid of the unseen and unknown by amplifying the perceived significance of the little things. If you hadn't sent Fear away, he would have condemned you to stay in the tent, causing you to neither go up the mountain or down it. You would have been stuck for God only knows how long. Many are caught in Fear's web and remain stagnant, not knowing Happiness or Success."

"Purpose, you said I would meet Failure along my quest to become one with you again. Failure is a friend of Success, and I was told he could introduce me if I listened to him. Isn't that the goal? Isn't that what everyone looks to achieve, Success? Surely if I meet Success, Happiness will follow?" Kevin asked the question for which most humans think they know the answer to.

"The human mind is as cunning as the universe is rigid. Happiness is everywhere, and bits of him live in all of us, including your positive allusions. You met Passion and you felt a bit of Happiness; you saw what Creativity could do and you felt a bit of Happiness; and you met me, and you felt a bit of Happiness. You met Gratitude, Love, Courage, Hope, and her four sisters and you felt Happiness. Humans become deceived by Fear, to be content with the little bits of Happiness that they get. They feel they can live off that because they fail to find me. Only I can take them to see Happiness, where they can unite to become one. But humans want things easy and so they stop and revel in the little bits of Happiness they find until it disappears one day."

Kevin thought of his mother. She had once been happy before his father had left them when Kevin was only a toddler.

"If people find Happiness through other means, why does he still abandon people knowing how much they need him?" Kevin questioned as they went along.

"Because they don't truly have Happiness. Happiness would never leave unless he was pushed away. Now this is where we must part ways Kevin. But trust me when I say that we will meet again," explained Purpose.

Kevin was suddenly aware of his surroundings. They were by the stairs that led to the foot of the mountain.

"But there is still so much I have to ask you; about me, about you," Kevin pleaded, reluctant to let go of Purpose.

"You know all that you need to know. What remains it to discover what you can do with what you know, and how far you can push yourself to become one with me as you were destined to be. Until we meet again always remember, you have all that you need inside of you."

With that, Purpose pulled his hand away from Kevin who tried to hold on but was unable. Purpose was gone in an instant.

"We will help you find Purpose again," Passion and Creativity chimed in unison.

Kevin: The Search for Happiness 1

Kevin returned to work with a smile on his face. Even though Passion had often refused to accompany Kevin to work, after coming down from the mountain, Passion escorted him now routinely. Contrary to Kevin's fears, people hardly gave Passion a second glance. He would sit at the farthest corners of the restaurant while Kevin tended to the customers at the counter.

After returning from the mountain, Kevin's job had become monotonous to him. One morning, a teenage girl came up to the counter. There was something familiar about her that made him pay attention. She walked with a slight limp, and she wore oversized sunglasses as though to hide her eyes.

"Morning Rachel," Kevin greeted her suddenly remembering her name as she often came to the restaurant with her friends in the evenings after school. She had never come to the restaurant at any other time of the day. Her shoulders sank as Kevin spoke to her and her body seemed to tremble. She adjusted her shades and shifted her weight onto her other leg, a series of movements to keep herself together.

"Why don't you go have a seat, I will order your usual," he told her, and she nodded a thank you and made her way feebly to her usual seat in the corner where Passion was seated.

Kevin handed the piece of paper with the girl's order on it, to one of the cooks. Thinking that the girl might like a cup of hot coffee; Kevin added this to her order. He had a feeling she would appreciate the small gesture.

"Just pass the tray to me when you're done. I will take care of it." His eyes never left the girl who sank into her seat looking warily at the people around her. No one seemed to pay her any mind, but soon enough her unease drew the unwanted attention she hoped to avoid. Kevin kept her order at his side while he tried to work quickly to make the queue in front of him disappear.

Seeing that the girl was soon to leave, he called one of the cooks to take over while he went to serve her.

"Don't leave yet, it's all here," he said to her with a bright smile that he hoped would calm her a little. The girl thanked him and straightened her posture to eat.

"I would advise the coffee first, you seem tired. It might liven you up a bit." She forced an awkward smile and picked up the cup of coffee.

"Thank you," she said. She seemed to have lost her voice.

Kevin didn't know what else to say to her. He had a strong feeling that something terrible had happened to the girl sitting opposite him and Passion. Passion nudged him to say something to the girl.

What would I say? Kevin thought. He was scared to say the wrong thing and set her off.

Anything, Passion mouthed inaudibly to him, *say anything.*

"What happened to you?" he asked her.

"I don't feel like talking about it," she answered rather harshly, but Kevin wasn't fazed.

"Was it your father?" He asked her. For a moment, it seemed he could see her eyes widen behind the sunglasses. She shook the table as she hurriedly stood up, but Kevin's hand found hers as though propelled by an instinct he had not known existed in him.

"I have been abused as well."

She hesitated, her countenance softened as she looked him over gauging his sincerity

"I was younger then. Sit, I may be able to help you."

Passion smiled at Kevin, *Good going there*, he mouthed as the girl slowly slid back into her seat. She pulled her hand out of Kevin's grasp and slowly removed the dark shades from her eyes. For a split second he could see that she had a black eye before she buried her face in her hands. She cried, muffling her sorrow with her hands.

"Why didn't you tell anyone?" he asked her.

"He said it was my fault for getting him angry, and that I deserved it," she sobbed through her hands.

"Hey, hey, look at me," Kevin pulled her hands away from her face gently, and she let him.

"You don't deserve any of this."

"I will take care of this," Passion said as he jumped off the seat to the floor. Kevin followed his quick movements as Purpose began a confrontation with the manager.

"What are you doing Kevin? I don't pay you to sit around and flirt with customers," the manager ranted. Kevin seemed distracted for a moment, thinking about his overdue bills and a life without a job. Passion continued in a heated conversation with the manager, but Kevin couldn't hear the words. The manager's face was in awe as he listened to Passion in their silent conversation. Kevin turned back to the girl, seeing there were no more distractions, and talked to her about her low self-esteem.

"Thank you," she said as she got up and gave him a hug. She held onto him longer than he had expected, but he accepted her gratitude. It made him feel good, not in his ability to turn a sad face into a glad one, but in the fact that she genuinely seemed happier. Her happiness was his happiness. She left promising to do as he had told her.

Kevin turned around and suddenly found himself standing where Passion had been, and Passion now stood by the door where Kevin had just been escorting the girl out of the restaurant—*they had swapped places.*

Before walking away calmly, Kevin's manager said, "I accept your resignation and wish you the best of luck following your Passion, Kevin." His manager seemed almost sad to see Kevin go.

Kevin wondered why he didn't feel the urge to beg the manager to take him back. Any other person would have been devastated about losing their major source of income without any other tangible alternative; but Kevin had a plan, and he had Passion and Creativity to help him execute it.

Walking out of the restaurant into a world with so many people and possibilities, Kevin turned to Passion.

"I told you that you would lose your job if I came along to work with you," Passion spoke sternly and raised his hands up in a show of no-blame.

Kevin smiled.

"I guess I knew it was going to happen. So, what now Passion? What course do we walk to find Purpose?"

"We are going to catch someone who's really fast and slippery," Passion offered eagerly with a smile that peaked Kevin's interest.

"Who is this fast and slippery person we have to catch?" Kevin was looking forward to meeting the person Passion spoke about with so much admiration.

"Oh, his name is Opportunity, and there is not a man in the world who can run faster than he can," Passion said as they came to a park.

"Do we catch him today?" Kevin asked eagerly.

"You could try, but it takes detailed planning to catch Opportunity. Today, I say just watch him, and then you can try to catch him."

***

All day Kevin and Passion sat on a bench in the park watching people pass. There were young and old people alike. They noted an elderly group of people that had gathered around an older man.

"Is that Opportunity?" Kevin asked Passion.

"No, Opportunity isn't that easy to spot. He is somewhere amongst the crowd, but even I cannot tell who he is. Be patient my friend, soon we will know."

"Are the rules of the game clear?" the elderly instructor asked of the group. Everyone clamored *Yes*. He clapped his hands and a younger man stepped away from the circle slowly. The instructor took out a tarnished whistle and blew it, and soon everyone was running around chasing one another.

"It's tag!" exclaimed Kevin, recognizing the game. He had watched other kids play the game when he was in elementary school. Some kids were good at it, as they had greater physical advantages than their peers. It wasn't the speed that really counted then, it was the simple act of having fun.

"Now, your first task is to find Opportunity before the game ends." Passion pointed to the alarm clock on the bench next to the elderly instructor. Kevin's eyes darted back to the game.

"Opportunity is one of the best players at this game. The only obstacle is that his appearance changes with each new game. Today he might be a man, tomorrow a woman, and the next day he may be a teenager. He can be anyone that suits him, and the best at scaping being tagged."

"As an onlooker, it's not so easy to spot him as everything seems chaotic. As a participant, it's much worse due to everyone running and moving about. Some people don't recognize Opportunity, so they just tag anyone with the hopes that no one will notice. In their thinking, they have achieved the goal of the game, tagging someone out; however, they never truly find the right Opportunity. You have to beware of those people."

Kevin saw a man tag person after person. He was fast, strong, agile and built like an athlete. *That must be Opportunity*, Kevin thought.

"No, he is one of those I spoke of. The ones who are blind to seeing who Opportunity really is. They become aimless and lose track of the objective of the game, which is—Tag!"

A young woman yelled as she tagged a man thinking she had caught Opportunity. Her aim wasn't to eliminate as many people from the game.

"While that is a fair enough strategy, had she been successful in tagging everyone else out, that still would have left her alone to contend with Opportunity." Kevin said.

"Perhaps, but he wasn't tagged by her. He kept going after random people and that left him defenseless," Passion stated.

They both watched the ejected man pick up a towel, wipe his face, and toss it away in anger. "I am not doing this again!" the man yelled as he walked away from the game.

"There are those who quit, and they are worse for it; while there are those who learn from their mistakes and try again."

"But they are not as fast as Opportunity. No matter the number of times they try, they can never catch him."

"This game isn't all about speed, Kevin. It appears that you do not see what I see. It requires endurance, wit, cunning, patience, and a strong will among other things. Have you never heard the saying that 'the race isn't given to the swift...'" Kevin nodded... "but to the strong." He had heard it many times before.

"Now, focus on finding Opportunity."

Kevin turned and faced the field squarely. He made a mental note of the best players out there. His eyes became fixed on a slender, athletic man who was outpacing everyone; dodging hands in his wake and jumping over obstacles as though they were his footstool. Soon, he was the only one being chased by a handful of people that remained in the game.

"I see him, there's Opportunity!" Kevin rejoiced.

"Excellent, you found him. What would you do next?"

"I shall catch him," Kevin said as he stood up and trotted off to meet the old instructor. He asked the man if he could still join the game.

"Yes, at any time anyone can join; but you only have 10 minutes left, son. I would advise that you return tomorrow for a new game," the old man instructed Kevin.

Kevin contemplated the idea, but he remembered what Passion had said. If he let the day go without participating, he would again have to figure out who Opportunity was the next day.

"Ten minutes is more than enough," Kevin answered and ran onto the field.

Five minutes in and he had fallen thrice already. Kevin removed his shoes and ran barefoot along the field. His feet hurt from the stones that were made hot by the sun's rays as it was positioned directly overhead at this time in the afternoon. Still, Kevin kept running, but he couldn't keep up with most of the players who chased behind Opportunity.

Suddenly, Opportunity fell, and a woman tagged him. Others rushed to tag her, but the instructor blew his whistle; *GAME OVER*. The instructor announced that the woman had won.

"It's so unfair," Kevin grumbled like most of the remaining people in the game as he walked back to join Passion.

"How so?"

"You saw it. I was terrible." Kevin sank onto the bench soaked in sweat and breathing hard. "I fell so many times and my feet hurt from not wearing the right shoes for running in. Look at how the game ended. Opportunity let her win. He could have easily dodged her outstretched hands, but he willingly fell so she could tag him. Favoritism, so unfair!"

"You lost because you were not prepared, Kevin. That woman won because she was quick to react after she saw Opportunity was down on the ground and vulnerable. You saw many people just quit while you were in the game even without getting tagged but she continued. She was prepared out there and in here." Passion pressed his pointy finger against his temple. "She deserved to win."

Passion stood up. "I guess we can come back again tomorrow."

"Let's stop at a sporting goods store on our way. I need to get new kicks," Kevin said, and Passion smiled with respect. He put his arm around Kevin's shoulder as they made their way out of the park.

***

"Wakey, wakey," Passion tapped Kevin as his alarm rang at 6:00 a.m.

"What time is it?"

Passion showed him the beeping time display on his phone.

Still groggy, Kevin nodded and hugged his pillow as he fell fast asleep again.

"Sorry about this, Kevin, but it must be done if we are to find Purpose," Passion said as he pulled Kevin off the bed onto the floor.

Minutes later, Kevin was wearing his new kicks and was jogging from his home to the park. He had asked Passion to come with him, but Passion had decided to stay at home.

"This is not my forte. You will find a better teacher to show you the ropes," Passion said.

Kevin grew tired as he made his way towards the park. The park was still a ways away and his legs were beginning to ache already.

"Excuse me," a man said as he brushed past Kevin. Watching the man jog ahead of him, Kevin realized it wasn't the first time the man had jogged past him that morning.

"Excuse me sir," Kevin called to the man. The man pulled out his earbuds and turned to Kevin, still jogging in one spot.

"Morning, how long have you been jogging?" asked the man.

"I doubt I have gone half as far as you have and I'm already beat," Kevin remarked.

"I've been out here for a while already, but I've got to keep moving, so sorry I can't stay and talk; talking consumes energy," the man said as he returned to his path. Kevin shrugged, not particularly offended by the man's curt response. Making a promise to himself to reach the park before the man passed him again, Kevin mustered up the strength and did just that.

The game hadn't begun yet, and this gave Kevin time to rest and grab a quick bite to eat. He was later joined by Passion. By this time, a crowd of people had gathered at the park. The instructor blew his whistle and they all circled around him.

"We all know the rules of the game. It's a simple game of tag." Everyone shared a laugh as the instructor continued, "the theme of the game, as we know it, is SEIZE THE OPPORTUNITY, good luck and happy tagging!"

The instructor blew his whistle and the game began. Kevin ran trying to evade others while he searched for Opportunity in the crowd. He could not tell how long he'd been running before his vision became blurry, he started seeing double, his legs buckled, and Kevin passed out.

When he awoke, he was laying on the bench next to Passion, who had an amusing smile on his face.

"How long was I out?" asked Kevin.

"Oh, just a few minutes, twenty perhaps," grinned Passion as he looked back to the field. Kevin's focus came back slowly.

"Who won?" asked Kevin with a puzzled look on his face.

Passion ignored Kevin's question and directed him to the café opposite the park; where others who lost the race gathered to complain.

Flustered, Kevin sat up and vented to Passion. He'd been coming to the park every day for two months to play tag and hadn't succeeded in winning.

"I am fed up, Passion. I wake up early every single morning, I jog to the park, then run all morning just so I can come here and lose! Maybe this is not the game for me. Not everyone has the talent for running, and some things you just cannot teach. It must be a natural gift. Perhaps we can try to catch Opportunity once he is done with the game."

Passion's face grew long as he listened to Kevin. All the talk about Opportunity concerned him.

"Why are you so sad?" Kevin asked Passion.

"Soon, you will not need me anymore," Passion replied.

"That's not true. You are my roommate now and my best friend," Kevin tried to reassure him, but it wasn't enough.

"Go see the man who speaks in the café and perhaps he might be able to help you."

Kevin nodded; eventually he stood up and headed for the café.

"Promise me you will be here when I return," Kevin pleaded with Passion.

"I will be here, if you still need me," Passion answered him and bid him on his way.

The closer Kevin got to the café, the clearer he could see the crowd inside. Some stormed out hissing and cursing as he approached. *This is the man Passion thinks can help me?* Kevin scoffed. Hesitant to go in, he walked by the glass door and looked in. Out of the crowd of people still dressed in their sweat soaked clothing, only about four were listening to the man. As Kevin gazed on, something about the man seemed familiar. As the man paused long enough to peer into the crowd that he noticed Kevin. It was Failure who smiled at the familiar face and waved for him to come to join them.

It is a stupid game. I can't do it anymore. What is the use of trying if you just can't catch Opportunity? Catch him you say, we don't even know what he/she looks like?

Kevin heard different statements of dejection as he entered. The aura inside the café was extremely negative. Everyone was grumbling and dissatisfied with one thing or another except the four people engrossed in their conversation with Failure.

"Hey Failure, we meet again," Kevin said as he came to join them. Failure shifted in his seat creating a space for Kevin.

"I knew we would see each other sooner or later. I only hope you will listen to me more this time than before."

Kevin's throat was dry, his legs ached, and his stomach rumbled with hunger. Without a job, he had not been eating well and the little he had, he shared with Passion.

"Opportunity isn't so difficult to catch. Follow these instructions, work on your weaknesses and persevere." They all thanked Failure and left the café much happier than the others who only spoke amongst themselves.

"Why did you lose?" Failure asked Kevin. Kevin seemed taken aback by the question.

"You gave them advice, why not me?" questioned Kevin.

"I didn't tell them anything they didn't already know. They came up with solutions on their own by looking back at their past failures and noticing their deficiencies. People see things differently when they let go of their weariness and just focus on forging ahead. What you heard was me simply reminding them of their own solutions."

Kevin tried to think back over the past two weeks, but he couldn't shake the fatigue and hunger that gripped him. All he wanted was to focus on catching Opportunity. Kevin closed his eyes as he recalled the many games of tag that he had participated in, "I do not have enough endurance."

Failure slapped the table with glee, "and there you have it!" Failure took out a piece of paper, scribbled an address on it, and passed it to Kevin.

"Be there at 5:00 a.m. and you will meet someone who can help you build up your endurance. Soon enough, you will be able to catch Opportunity." Kevin got up and thanked Failure.

"It wasn't so bad talking with you," Kevin admitted.

"Good, just do yourself a favor and don't allow these people's negativity to get to you while you eat. They might drown you in their lack of will," advised Failure before leaving Kevin in the café.

Passion was still sitting on the bench when Kevin returned to the park.

"You didn't leave!" Kevin exclaimed with joy.

"You still need me," Passion answered with a smile as they headed home.

***

Kevin was at the address Failure had given him by 4:30 a.m., 30 minutes before he had been told to arrive.

"You're here early, that's a good sign. It shows strong will and determination, I can work with that," a voice said from behind him. Kevin turned to see the man whom he frequently met while jogging. The man was well built and at peak fitness. He walked as he talked, and Kevin could hardly keep up with his stride.

"Forgive me, I should introduce myself. I am Determination, and together we shall get you into tip top shape for the game."

Kevin trained with Determination for weeks and kept to a new diet as instructed. Soon he was able to run with endurance like Determination.

"When do you think I will be ready?" Kevin asked Determination on the fourth week.

"You have always been ready Kevin. You only needed to have the confidence to go back and try," Determination told him.

"How long have you been jogging?" Kevin asked as they walked to the park.

"Since I can remember. I just can't help myself, pushing myself further and further every day," Determination answered. "I never stop until I accept my set target."

When they got to the park, they met a large crowd ready to play tag.

"Where are you going?" Kevin asked Failure as they arrived.

"I'll be back after the game is over, I'm not needed for now. He turned to Determination, "Do you think he is ready?"

"It is up to him," Determination answered. Kevin was slightly dejected by the lack of faith that Determination had in him, but that only spurred him on to prove himself even more.

The game began and Kevin ran as if his life depended on it. He was much faster and agile than he had been the last time he had seen Failure. Players fell, gave up, and fainted; but Kevin kept running after Opportunity, a middle-aged woman with white canvas shoes. Soon, it was only the two of them on the field. Opportunity was slippery, dodging Kevin's every lunge, but Kevin kept coming. With one wrong turn, Opportunity paused momentarily, and Kevin was able to tag him.

Failure, Passion, and Creativity rushed the playing field to join Kevin as the game came to an end. Kevin had been so focused that he had not noticed when his friends arrived at the park.

"Now that you have won, you should come and claim your prize. You will need your friends there too," Opportunity said revitalized.

Opportunity hailed a taxi, and they all got in except for Kevin and Failure.

"What about your friend Success?" Kevin asked Failure.

"You're in good hands with Opportunity, he will take you to Success. The time has come for us to go our separate ways Kevin; I hope we do not meet again," Failure said as he waved goodbye and walked away. Kevin turned and entered the taxi.

Opportunity took them to a tall building. There were many people inside dressed in suits, walking about doing one task or another. She led Kevin, Passion, and Creativity to a small office. Inside was a small wooden table, and a metal desk with three big hammers on it.

"Your task is to break down the walls that block your access to Purpose and Success," Opportunity told them before leaving.

"Let's start smashing walls then, shall we?" Passion said to Kevin.

What should have taken several months, only took weeks due to Passion and Kevin's determination, as well as Creativity being stronger than she appeared. As the last remaining wall crumbled to pieces, Kevin ran into Purpose's arms.

"I found you," Kevin said, out of breath. When Kevin finally pulled away, Purpose introduced him to the man next to him. He was slightly older than Kevin, perhaps in his early forties, had a clean-shaven face and was dressed in a shiny suit. He extended his hand to Kevin.

"Hello Kevin, Purpose has told me a lot about you. We have been eagerly waiting for you to break through the wall, I am Success."

Kevin: The Search for Happiness 2

"Help, help!" yelled Kevin, but his screams were muffled by the gray tape that held fast to his mouth. The night before, he had been kidnapped by a masked man on his way to an awards ceremony. Minutes later, he was in a dark basement bound and gagged. The sound of a door opening somewhere above told him that his kidnapper was coming for him. He heard the man flip the switch on the wall as the dangling light bulb came to life. The bulb was so close to Kevin's face that he could not see much else.

The masked man pulled up a chair and sat opposite of Kevin. He pulled undid the gag so Kevin could speak.

"What do you want from me? I am successful; I can get you whatever you need," Kevin pleaded. In one swift movement, the kidnapper pulled the bulb away from Kevin, redirected it towards himself, and removed his mask. Kevin was shocked by the face that was now staring back at him; it was his face! Illuminated now, Kevin could see that his lookalike was dressed in the suit he had worn the night before for the ceremony. It was the exact same suit he had seen Success wear about a year before.

"Yes, the thoughts that are formulating in your head are true. But before you let your imagination go too far, let me introduce myself. I am Self, but most people call me Pride."

"Why do you have me here? What did I ever do to you?" Kevin pleaded.

"You woke me from my slumber, Kevin. Imagine my surprise to find a man impersonating me," Pride said as he stood to his feet. Leaving the bulb to dance on its own cord, Pride walked past Kevin and switched on a television behind him, allowing ambient light to fill the room. He repositioned Kevin so he could watch the television. Kevin saw Pride in his suit at the ceremony accepting the award and reveling in the attention he received from the cameras, models, and fans at the ceremony.

"You go out as me, and you insult me!" Pride shouted into Kevin's ears.

"That is not me getting all the glory, it is you!" Kevin belted back, angry that someone else had taken his spot.

"Well, it sure looks like you," Pride said as he turned Kevin back to facing the light. Pride stomped back up the stairs towards the door.

"Please set me free," Kevin begged, fearing what Pride would do to him.

"Promise that you will never credit my glory for yours. The deeds you do and the happiness you bring to people's faces need to serve a higher purpose. Embrace Purpose and leave the spotlight to me. You didn't achieve all this by yourself Kevin; you had help. You cannot afford to be me!" Pride shouted from the top of the stairs before he slammed the door closed behind him.

The room was suddenly immersed in light, and Kevin saw Purpose tied to a chair next to him. Kevin squirmed in his chair trying to free himself so he could also free Purpose, but the ropes were too tight.

He thought about what Pride had said. There was truth in his words. Over time, Kevin had forgotten the feeling that pulsated through his body the first time he had spoken to the girl at the restaurant. All he had thought about recently was partying and spending time with Success. He had neglected Purpose, Passion and Creativity. He had become full of himself, his ability, and his achievements. He had started impersonating Pride without even knowing it.

"I remember, Pride! I am sorry for being you. I shall never be you again!" Kevin shouted at the top of his voice. He heard the door open and Pride descended the stairs.

"Do you swear? Because if I see you impersonating me again, I will come find you," Pride threatened Kevin.

"I promise." Replied Kevin earnestly. Pride cut him loose and Purpose as well. Kevin hugged Purpose and apologized for not protecting him and for neglecting him.

"All that matters is that we are free and together again," Purpose assured him. Purpose took Kevin by the hand and led him up the stairs. "There is one more person you need to meet upstairs."

They climbed the stairs solemnly and came out of a door that opened directly into a ceremony of some sort. They were greeted and shown to a table. The guests were well off and beautifully dressed.

"You will soon be called up, so go freshen up in the bathroom," Purpose told him. Kevin wiped his sweaty face with his handkerchief and made his way to the bathroom. He entered, turned open the tap at the sink, and splashed cold water onto his face. As Kevin washed his face, he glanced at himself in the mirror. The reflection he saw was that of a slightly younger and happier image of himself.

"Hello Kevin," the smiling man in the mirror beamed. Kevin leaned closer to the mirror.

"Who are you?" Kevin asked the reflection.

"I am you, Kevin, and you can call me Happiness."